DETROIT PUBLIC LIBRARY

P9-CDS-195

Bad Choices CAN BE DEADLY

Monica Lynne Foster

CHASE BRANCH LIBRARY
17731 W. SEVEN MILE RD.
DETROIT, MI 48235
313-481-1580

MAY 1 7

CH

Bad Choices Can Be Deadly
Copyright © 2014 Monica Lynne Foster
All rights reserved.

Published by
ML Foster Empowerment Group
PO BOX 700529
Plymouth, MI 48170

This is a work of fiction. The names, characters, places, and incidents within are the products of the author's imagination or are used fictitiously, and any resemblance to actual persons, living or dead, business establishments, events, or location is entirely coincidental. The publisher does not have any control over and does not assume any responsibility for author or third-party websites or their content.

No part of this book may be reproduced, scanned, or distributed in any printed or electronic form without permission. Please do not participate in or encourage piracy of copyrighted materials in violation of the author's rights. Purchase only authorized editions.

If you purchase this book without a cover, you should be aware that this book is stolen property. It was reported as "unsold and destroyed" to the publisher, and neither the author nor the publisher has received any payment for this "stripped book."

Cover and Interior Design By
TWA Solutions
www.twasolutions.com

ISBN: 978-0-9965825-1-3

For inquiries, contact the publisher.

Dedication

This novel is dedicated to my precious grandmother,

Visel S. Nervis

January 5, 1913—April 14, 2013

I still love you with all of my heart...

Discover Other Titles by
Monica Lynne Foster

THE CHANELLE SERIES
Hands Off My Man – Book 2

INSPIRATION
Today Is Your Last Day...Say Wha?!
(The first 24 months after you lose your job)

Amazon Author Profile and Full Book List:
amazon.com/author/monicalynnefoster

Monica's Official Website and Social Media
www.monicalynnefoster.com
https://twitter.com/mlfoster5
http://www.facebook.com/booksbymonicalynnefoster

Thanks from Monica

I have so many to thank for my labor of love, but, above all else, I thank God. My Heavenly Father has blessed me with a gift for writing and a very active imagination. It's taken me over 11 years to complete my novel, but I believe that now is the appointed time for it to be introduced to the world.

I thank my precious grandmother, Visel Nervis. My grandmother celebrated 100 years of life on January 5, 2013 and she left us to join her husband and the Lord on April 14, 2013. As a gift to me, she left me with savings bonds that she purchased when I was a toddler. I sat on them for over a year because I wanted to honor her memory. What better way to honor my grandmother's legacy than to bring my life's dream to fruition and have it be around for eternity?

I thank my husband and partner in this journey called life, Keith Foster. There is no one on this planet who I'd rather be with on this journey. I love love love my husband. You nurture and support me in my dreams, some of which can be a little "out there" and I'm grateful. I'm a visual writer, meaning that I have to visualize the scene before I can pen it. And I thank you for acting out scenes with me so I could later write them down! Not many men would do that and I know you do it because you love me.

Thank you to my mom, Visel Jeanne Franklin. My mom is the absolute best! My mother has supported me and my ideas my entire life. I remember calling her when I was in my early 20's and telling her that I quit my good paying job to sell T-shirts at a kiosk during summer festivals (which by the way I never did). I'm sure my mom prayed behind my back, but to my face she helped with T-shirt designs. I like to joke that if I wanted to sell popsicles to Eskimos, my mom would be my first investor.

Thank you to my entire family and extended family, Aunt Linda, Aaron, Jalen, Aeryn, Tyler, Tyrel, Naomi, Crystal, Eileen, Heather, Sylvia, Terry, Tracee, Taylor, Aunt Doris, Uncle Shaw, Ron, Cheyenne, DJ, Dee, Neal, Julian, Kenneth Christopher, Shirley, Ouma, Dianna, Kathryn, and Benny to name a few. You love me and let me be me. I know I can be over the top at times, but you just roll your eyes and continue to support me.

Thank you to my circle of women friends. Some part of each of you can be seen in the bestie in the book. Cheryl Williams, thank you for showing me a positive marriage and giving me something to hope for before I had it. Tammie Rich, thank you for being more than my friend. You are my sister and you would do some of the crazy things my two female characters did. Actually, we have done some ridiculous things in the past, but now isn't the time to discuss them. Nicole Burrell, thank you for being a friend who will listen to me complain and still answer my call the next day! Crystal Gillery, thank you for being such an example of a strong woman. You stand tall in your convictions, even if you stand alone, and I draw strength from you. Lyn Roberts, thank you for showing me how to be laid back with my husband. I love how you don't have to raise your voice to get your point across.

Thank you to my Sorors of Delta Sigma Theta and, in particular, my line sisters, the 11 Inquisitors, Christina Gilbert, and my purse Tamika A. Frimpong. I love you all for being positive examples of women. Thank you to Jamillah Carpenter. It's hard to believe we've been friends for 20 years! You always bring a smile to my face. Thank you to Stephanie Merck. You are one of the only friends that I can talk to for hours on end and still have more to say the next day. You have no idea how much you encouraged me when you would read my draft and ask about the next chapter, and I hadn't even written it yet! Thank you to Tascha Moses. We have been through a lot and it's strengthened our friendship in ways I could have never imagined. Thank you to Minister Ardella Darst, my friend, and mentor. It was an amazing experience for me to work under you during my days in the corporate world. Thank you to Vickie Hall, Cindy Pool, Maia Cross, Shawn Jones, and Monica Benford-Echols. I am blessed to call each of you my friend for life.

Special thanks to Victoria Christopher Murray, my mentor and friend. The blessing you've been to my life is indescribable. And to Jessica Wright Tilles, with TWA Solutions, for my bomb cover. You nailed it!

And thank you to my readers. It is my sincere prayer that this novel is just the beginning of many to come and that you will share this experience with me.

To anyone I may have missed, please forgive me. I'll catch you on my second book, the sequel to *Bad Choices Can Be Deadly* and the second in the Chanelle Series.

#

I dropped the handle of my suitcase. "What are you doing?" I screamed to my boyfriend of 12 years as he scrambled to cover himself and I picked up my emergency baseball bat by the side of my bed.

"Chanelle! Chanelle! I can explain."

I swung the bat and lucky for him he ducked, because the whack of the bat put a nice size dent in my headboard. "You can't possibly explain this!" My eyes had to be betraying me. There was no way I'd just come home from a business trip and found the love of my life in our bed with his personal trainer. His male personal trainer.

"Honest to God, Chanelle, this isn't what it looks like!" He held his arms out in front of him, in a futile attempt to block the inevitable future swing of my get-even tool.

"Don't you dare bring God into your sordid mess! It's exactly what it looks like! How could I have been so stupid to trust you and give you 12 years of my life! 12! Ugh!" I said, as I swung again, missing him, but connecting with my lamp. Then I turned my fury on Rocco. "And you! I welcomed you into my home!"

"It's not my fault you can't give him what I can," the home wrecker taunted me.

"Not now, Rocco," Michael yelled.

We'd been together long enough for Michael to know what I was capable of doing, and at this moment, I was thinking I could handle a 20-year bid at the state prison. "Get out! Both of you get out!"

They jumped out of the bed without a stitch of clothing and bent down to pick up their pants.

"No! You don't get to put on clothes," I continued shouting, while brandishing my bat.

"Chanelle, it's winter and it's freezing outside," my now ex pleaded.

"You say that like I care! You have exactly one second to be out of my house or I swear to God, I'm gonna catch a case. Now go!"

I chased them down the steps and out my front door. Watching them run butt naked and barefoot down the snowy street of my posh subdivision was suddenly comical. And I began laughing. I sat on the porch and laughed until I cried. But the tears of humor quickly turned to tears of pain as the betrayal set in. Pain that what I thought was a solid relationship was really a sham. Pain that I'd wasted years of my life with a man who could never be committed to me. Pain that I was now... alone.

Chapter 1
One Month Later

"Michael, what are you doing here?" I said when I opened my door and saw my ex standing on my porch...with his new lover.

"We're here to give you this," he said, handing me a piece of paper.

I looked at it trying to make out what I was reading. "What is it?"

"You've been served."

"Excuse me?"

"You heard me."

"You're *suing* me?"

"He's not," his lover chimed in, while holding Michael's hand. "I am."

"This must be a joke."

"It's no joke, missy. I'll see you in court," the man stealer said, whipping his neck around as though he had long hair instead of a bald head.

I turned on Michael. "And you're just going to stand here and let him do this to me? Like I never meant anything to you?" I screamed, waving the paper that cemented his betrayal.

"Chanelle, you burned all of my stuff. Everything I owned. So yeah, I'm behind Rocco on this."

I thought about the bonfire I'd had right after his breach of trust. He was right. I set everything he had ablaze. Even got a fine from the city because of the fire. But it was worth it when he showed up with the moving truck the following day and I handed him pictures of ashes. It would make more sense if *he* was suing me. But Rocco? What did I do to him?

I watched Rocco and the man I once loved with everything in me walk down my steps and get into their car. Then I groaned and shut the door on a chapter of my life that was closed forever.

"Hurry up! We're going to be late!" I said to my best friend, Michele. I loved her like a sister, but she was incredibly slow when we were kids and nothing had changed.

"Where are you going tonight, Auntie Chanelle?" I looked into the eyes of my four-year-old godson Benjamin Jr. and melted, as usual.

"Well, I've been invited to a holiday party for my job and your mom is going with me."

"But it's January. Christmas is over."

"You're very smart, BJ. You're right. Christmas is over. But sometimes companies celebrate after Christmas."

He frowned. "That doesn't make sense."

He was right again, and I wished the party had been canceled. But it was a tradition in our company to celebrate the holidays in January, whether we wanted to or not. So I said, "It doesn't make sense to me either. But sometimes grownups have to do things they don't want to do."

"Oh…well, who's going to watch me and read me my bedtime story?"

I smiled at Benjamin, Jr. "Now BJ, who usually reads you your bedtime story when Mommy is gone?"

"Daddy."

"So, don't you think Daddy will read you your story tonight and put you to bed?"

"Yessss, but I want Mommy to do it."

"You want Mommy to do what?" Michele asked, walking into the family room.

"I want you to read a story to me," BJ whined.

Now I loved my godson, but I didn't have time for this. As it was, we were going to be late.

"Sweetie, how about letting Daddy read to you tonight, and I'll read you a story tomorrow night?" Michele offered.

"Okay, Mommy, if you read me two stories tomorrow night."

I couldn't believe they were negotiating, but whatever it took to get us out of here was fine with me.

"It's a deal. Can Mommy have a kiss?"

Michele bent down and BJ ran into his mother's arms. She scooped him up and deposited him into his father's lap. "We should be back around 11:00 honey," she said, giving Benjamin, Sr. a light kiss on the lips.

"Okay, baby. You two have fun." He smiled at his wife.

"We will," she said, gazing back at him.

Benjamin Sr. looked at me. "Don't get my wife into any trouble. I know how you two can be when you're together."

"Whatever, Ben. Michele is the one who's the bad influence!"

We laughed as Michele grabbed her purse, coat, and keys. And then we left.

Once inside my BMW sedan, Michele turned on Watercolors, the Jazz station on satellite radio, and we drove in silence, each of us lost in our separate thoughts.

"So, are you okay with this?" Michele asked.

"Okay with what?"

"Don't play with me, Chanelle. This is the first time you've gone out since you and Michael broke up. I know you haven't told anyone about it and people are bound to be curious when you show up with me as your date. So how are you with this?"

"Well, I'm okay. I mean, I have to be. What choice do I have? I thought Michael was my soul mate and I thought we'd be together forever. But that turned out not to be the case. He decided he wanted to spend his life with someone who can give him something I never can. And by the way, his new boyfriend is suing me."

"You're kidding! For what?"

"Get this. Frostbite. When I kicked them out of my house. Correction. When I kicked them out of my *bed*, without clothes, they had to walk to Rocco's house. I guess his little goodies got too cold and he had to be hospitalized. He's coming after me for his medical bills."

"Unbelievable."

"Tell me about it."

"Let me know the court date and I'll go with you. And I'm not worried about Rocco. I know you'll handle him. But you still haven't *really* told me if you're okay with your breakup with Michael."

Sometimes I hated the fact that she knew me so well.

I took a long pause. "I had a decision to make and I made it. But no, I am not okay. Is that what you want to hear? I thought I'd have a family, a white picket fence, and even a dog at this stage in my life, and I don't have any of those things. For the first time ever, I am truly by myself. I've let my 20's and half of my 30's pass me by. And now I have to start over. I'm alone. And I'm scared. I'm in a society where almost everyone is part of a couple and I'm not. I'm on my way to a holiday party for work and you're my date! I am not okay and yet I have to pretend that I am. And on top of everything else, I got dumped by a guy who was on the down low. And I missed it." I let out a huge sigh after finishing my soliloquy. "Are you satisfied?"

Michele raised her eyebrows and responded. "Actually, I am, because this is the first time you've been honest with me. But, more importantly, it sounds like this is the first time you've been honest with yourself. Sweetie, you'll be okay. God has someone incredible for you. Just be patient. Take this time to get to know you all over again."

"I hear ya. It's just…" I paused. I felt the tears welling up and threatening to spill over and now was not the time. "It's just, I'm really, really scared to be by myself. And I'm more scared to start dating again."

"That's natural. You shouldn't even be thinking about dating yet."

"But if I don't date, then how will I meet the man that God has for me?"

"You'll meet him when you're whole. When the time is right," Michele answered.

I rolled my eyes. "Leave it to a happily married woman to have some lame response like that."

"Hey, you know as well as I do, that Ben and I weren't always in a good space. We had to work like hell to stay together."

I thought about what she said. She and Ben had been together forever, but there was a time, earlier in their marriage, when he'd had a severe gambling problem. Michele had threatened to divorce him if he didn't clean up his act. He knew she was serious and checked into a gambler's rehab program. Thankfully, it worked and with counseling and prayer, their marriage was stronger than it had ever been. But I didn't see the same fairy tale ending in my future, so I said, "Yeah, yeah, whatever. I don't wanna talk about this anymore, and besides that, we're here." I pulled up to the front of the hotel and waited for the valet to open my door. He handed me a ticket and Michele and I went inside to the grand ballroom.

The room was breathtaking with its white cathedral ceilings and 4-tiered crystal chandeliers sprinkled throughout. Each table was covered in cream linen with fine china place settings and tabletop poinsettias as centerpieces. Red, white, and gold floral arrangements were placed on either side of the dance floor, the bar, and the dessert tables. All the chairs were wrapped in red cloth with bows tied behind the chair backs. The DJ on the stage was playing soft holiday dinner music, and a handful of couples were already enjoying themselves on the dance floor.

"Good evening, may I take your coats for you?" the host asked, while looking at me.

"Thank you." I slid my burgundy full-length mink with the fox trim from my shoulders and into the waiting hands of the host. Michele, the animal activist of our group, did the same with her full-length faux black mink. Another host escorted us to our table.

As we walked, I knew we were drawing attention. Not that I was conceited, but I knew that I was blessed. I was used to standing out in a crowd and tonight was no exception. I had on a deep burgundy floor length evening gown that crisscrossed in the back and had a plunging neckline. The strappy heels and matching purse of the same color completed my outfit. And my hair, which usually fell below my shoulders, was worn in an up do with a few tendrils left out to frame my face.

Michele was doing her thing in a black dress that barely skimmed her knees and hugged her curves. With her hair cascading down her back in big full curls, she strutted in her 6-inch Louboutin's as though they were flats.

As we reached our table, I noticed Sean and my stomach did a somersault. If there was any man who could help me get over Michael, it was Sean. But he was married, which made him off limits.

Sean was a marketing consultant for our company, a technology business that had survived the tech nosedive. We were thriving and a great deal of our success was due to the work of Sean's firm. They'd done an outstanding job of helping us market our products and position us as an industry leader. Anytime we had a company function, Sean was invited. He was around so much that sometimes we forgot he wasn't an actual employee.

Though we worked together, I'd never checked him out. But since my breakup, I'd been paying closer attention and I liked what I saw. Except for the fact that he had a Mrs.

But *oooh*, he was gorgeous! Milk chocolate brown and 6 feet of solid muscle. And he had to wear at least a size 13 shoe. Hmmm… I wondered if there was any correlation… I had to admonish myself for the thought. I found myself having these thoughts often and it was bothering me. I knew better and yet…

Anyway, we arrived at our table and allowed the host to pull out our chairs. Sean was such a gentleman that he stood until we were comfortably seated. Since we were the only four at the table, I put my thoughts in check. "Hi Sean. Hi Cynthia. It's lovely to see you this evening," I said, engaging in the dinner chitchat that I loathed. "I'd like to introduce you to my best friend, Michele." I made the introductions and smiled politely.

Michele extended her hand. "It's nice to meet you."

"Likewise," the Mrs. said. Something about her demeanor had always disturbed me. Cynthia then turned her attention to me. "So, where's Michael this evening?"

She continued to remind me why I didn't like her. But rather than tap dance around the issue, I addressed it, so we could move on. "Actually, Cynthia, we are not together anymore." *Because he's banging his trainer*, I thought.

"Awww…that's too bad," she feigned sympathy. "He was so sweet. What did you do to run him away?"

My eyes narrowed and I clinched my teeth. I couldn't believe she'd said that! Judging by the crimson color that had settled in his cheeks, neither could Sean. He opened his mouth to speak, but I beat him to it. "You're right. Michael is a very sweet man, which is why we are able to remain friends," I lied. "But sometimes two people can outgrow each other."

Before the conversation had a chance to continue, Benson Jeffries, the firm's CEO, and his wife Phoebe, arrived at the table.

"Chanelle, it's great to see you!" Mr. Jeffries took my hand and put it to his lips.

He was such a charmer. He tried insisting that I call him Benson, but given that he was about 40 years my senior, I couldn't do it. "Hello, Mr. Jeffries."

After the second round of introductions, we had non-eventful conversation throughout dinner. Cynthia didn't say anything else rude, which was surprising. Immediately following dinner, she received a phone call and excused herself. Michele also left the table to check on BJ, and the Jeffries hit the dance floor, which left Sean and me.

"Dinner was great," Sean said.

"I thought so too!" I replied, sounding like the nerd who was complimented by the high school jock.

"So, how's the new proposal coming?"

"Pretty good." I was working on a proposal for a multi-million dollar account that we were pitching in the upcoming weeks. Sean had been giving me some suggestions, for which I was grateful. "I'm pulling together the final projections, which are a little harder to develop than I had anticipated." If I landed this account, I was sure to make partner.

"Well, let me know if I can be of any more assistance. From what I've seen, I think you're on the right track."

"Thanks. If you truly mean that, then I'd love for you to take a look at the final presentation before I present it to Mr. Jeffries."

"I really mean it. I'll review it for you," Sean offered.

Just then, Cynthia returned to our table. "Honey, I have to leave. An emergency came up at the hospital and I need to be there."

I wondered what kind of emergency came up at a pet hospital that the on-call vet couldn't handle. Or maybe she was the on-call vet.

"Can't Dave handle it?" Sean asked. "I thought he was on-call tonight?" That answered that question.

"Oh…well… he's really not equipped." Was that light mist on her forehead perspiration? I wondered as she continued. "I'd feel better if I were there."

"O…K…" He didn't seem to be buying her story either. "Let me get our coats."

"Oh, no. Don't bother. I'll take a taxi."

"Why? Don't you want me to take you? Especially if you're in a hurry."

I wondered how she was going to answer. I wished I'd had some popcorn, because this show was getting good.

"I-I-I know this is work for you. I'll be fine."

"Well, then at least take the car. I'll catch a taxi."

After a brief hesitation, she finally relented. "Okay. I don't have time to argue with you." She kissed him on the cheek and scurried out the door.

Wow, was all I could think. And if he believed her story, then I had a bridge I'd build and sell him.

After she left, the air around us was a little tense: I diverted my eyes, not wanting to look at Sean.

Across the room, Michele was in the corner still on the phone. She was smiling and twirling her hair. Ben must have been reminding her how good it was to be married. I knew she would be ready to get home soon, and though I was happy for her, I had to admit that I was a little envious.

"So, would you like to dance?" Sean politely asked, cutting right through my thoughts.

I was stunned by his question, so it took me a second to answer. They were playing the Isley Brother's *"Spend the Night,"* which happened to be one of my favorites.

"Sure," I said as nonchalantly as I could, hoping he couldn't tell that I was shaking slightly.

My heart went from 0 to 60 as he took my hand and led me to the dance floor. I kept telling myself to get it together. This was a dance with a friend. A married friend. Nothing more. Nothing less.

Once we stepped onto the floor, he wrapped his strong arms around me and I leaned against his chest. I inhaled the scent of his masculine cologne and closed my eyes, doing my best to pretend that it was okay for me to be here dancing with him. And I had to pretend hard because I knew better. I was really going to have to repent tonight. But in the meantime, I let myself surrender to the moment.

We didn't talk, we simply danced. And we danced. And we danced. Then the DJ picked up the pace and played some classic Motown. We started doing some of the old school dances like the "Twist" and "Mashed Potatoes", which made us and those around us laugh. "You're really a good dancer." He had to practically shout over the music.

"So are you."

"Don't laugh, but my mother made me take lessons when I was a kid and I really got into it."

"So did mine. I took lessons from the time I could walk until 12th grade."

I'd completely forgotten that Michele was my date until she approached us. "Hey, Twinkle Toes, I hate to bust your groove, but I told my husband I would be home by 11:00 and it's 11:30. I have my own groove that I'd like to get started, if you know what I mean."

I knew exactly what she meant and I was jealous. Arrgh, I hated the single life!

"Okay. Let me finish out this song and then we'll go," I answered.

"Cool. I'll get our coats."

After Michele walked off, I said to Sean, "I had a great time."

"Me too." He looked like he didn't want the night to end, and I had to admit that I didn't either, so I asked him, "Do you want a ride home?"

"Thanks, but I don't want to be a bother."

"It's no bother. Really."

"Well, if you're sure, then thanks." We said our goodbyes, then he received his coat from the coat check and the three of us headed to the valet to wait for my car. After giving me his address, which I plugged into the car navigation system, we chatted on our way to his home since he was the first to be dropped off.

When we stopped in front of his house, he said, "Thanks for the ride. Have a good night, ladies."

"You too," we said in unison.

He exited the car and walked up the steps. I waited until he was in the house before driving off. Then I waited to hear Michele's mouth. And she didn't disappoint me.

"We'll talk about this tomorrow. Right now, I have my husband on the brain and I can't wait to get home."

"I don't want to talk about this." And I didn't. I honestly didn't.

"I know, but we're going to anyway," Michele replied. We arrived at her house a few moments later. "Thanks, I had fun."

"Thanks for going with me," I responded.

As Michele opened the door and swung her legs out, she turned back to me and said, "Chanelle, be careful. You're playing a dangerous game."

"I know," was all I could say.

"I'll call you tomorrow. Love you."

"Love you too," I said to her before she closed the door. As I drove off, I hoped and prayed that thoughts of Sean would not invade my sleep. But I knew they would.

Chapter 2

"Hello?" I grumbled, sounding like I'd swallowed Kermit the Frog.

"Good morning, Sunshine!" Michele said, calling me by my childhood nickname. "Are you still in bed?"

"What do you think? And why are you so perky?" I kept my head under the covers and hoped this would be a brief conversation so I could go back to sleep.

"I don't see how you can sleep so late. It's almost 9:00. I've been up for hours. I've even been to the grocery store."

I feigned excitement. "Wow! So you're superwoman. Big deal."

"My, my. Someone woke up on the wrong side of the bed."

"That's my point. I'm not trying to be awake yet. I've got one more hour of sleep before I have to get ready for church. Now, if you don't mind, I'd like to get back to Morris Chestnut."

"I can't believe you. How you can have these dreams and then go to church?"

"It gives me something to repent about. See you in a couple of hours. Bye." I hung up before Michele had a chance to say anything else.

I squeezed my eyes shut and prayed for sleep to come back to me, but it was useless. I was awake. Reluctantly, I rolled out of bed. I went to the balcony door off the side of my bedroom and pulled back the curtains to let in the daylight. I cracked the door about an inch and felt the crisp winter air.

With a sudden burst of energy, I went downstairs to the kitchen and brewed a fresh pot of Kona coffee. As my coffee percolated, I walked into my family room and popped in my yoga DVD. After a quick workout, I enjoyed my coffee and a bagel, then headed upstairs to get dressed.

I was ready in under 40 minutes and called Michele as I walked out to my attached three-car garage. "Hey girl, you guys doin' the family thing or you want a ride?"

"Yeah, swing by. Ben went to early service since he has to be at work at noon today. Two employees called in, so he's got to cover their routes."

"No problem. See you in a few." I hopped into the driver's seat of my burnt orange Range Rover and backed out of the garage. Whenever I picked up my godson or my niece, I drove my Rover. They said it was the coolest ride ever.

As I pulled up to Michele's house, BJ came running out. "Auntie! Auntie!"

"Hey baby! Where's Mommy?"

"She forgot her purse so she went back to get it." He opened the back door, sat in his car seat that I kept in his spot, and fastened his seatbelt without any help. He was already four and growing into a big boy right before my eyes.

"Hey, girl," Michele said, checking BJ's harness then closing his door before getting into the passenger seat.

"Wassup?"

"Andrea, your favorite sister. She said she called you but you didn't answer. Rachel needs a ride to church this morning."

"Rachel is *her* daughter. Why can't she take her?" My sister did this kind of stuff all the time. I checked my phone and there were no missed calls.

"She's not feeling well, so she isn't going this morning."

"Mm-hmm. I wonder if Dante has anything to do with how she's feeling." Dante was my sister's on-again, off-again, good for nothing baby's daddy. They'd been together for 18 years! The only good thing that had come from their relationship was my niece.

"She didn't say. All she said was that Rachel needed a ride and could you pick her up."

Michele hated to get involved when it came to Andrea, who was five years older than us, but she acted like she was ten years younger. I swear my sister was allergic to responsibility.

"What choice do I have? Call her and let her know we're on our way."

"I already told her you would do it."

I smacked my lips. "What if I'd said no?"

"In the 11 years that Rachel has been on this earth, have you ever said no?" Michele challenged.

"Yeah, yeah. That child is my weakness. So anyway, how was your evening?" I asked, changing the subject.

Michele's grin broke into a wide smile as memories of her night came rushing back to her. "Girrlll…that brotha is gifted. And he's like the energizer bunny. He just kept going and going and going and going. And he went all night. I don't know what got into him."

"I do. It was that dress. You were a hottie!"

"Whatever!" she said, giving me a playful push.

"I'm serious. You were workin' it. He was drooling before you even left the house."

"He went all out. He turned our bedroom into a romantic retreat. He must have put BJ to bed right after we left." She stopped talking long enough to glance back at her son, who had become one with the DVD he was watching on the TV that I'd installed in the back of the headrest. "Anyway, he had jasmine-scented candles everywhere in the bedroom and he even had the tub filled with water and baby oil and get this, he had rose petals floating across the top."

"No!"

"Yes!" Michele continued. I looked over at her and though her body was in the passenger seat, her mind had clearly returned to last night. "From the front of the tub to the back were dozens of rose petals. And you know what was playing in the background.

"Not the Isley Brothers?

"You know it. *Spend the Night.* That did it. When I walked into the bedroom he was laying on the bed with that silk robe I bought him in Japan. He slid off the bed and came to me and kissed me like he did when we first started dating."

"Keep talkin'." I prompted her.

Michele recapped the rest of her evening and shared details that only best friends could talk about. "When he told me I was the most beautiful woman he'd ever seen, I cried. He kissed away my tears and the rest was history..." Michele's eyes misted a little.

"Awww... that was so sweet. I'm stuck on him putting rose petals in the bathtub."

"Girlll, it was the most unbelievable experience we've ever had. Although, today he's picking up a bottle of drain cleaner because the rose petals clogged the tub. Oops."

We both laughed. It was sad that my love life had to be lived through Michele, but it was all I had for the moment.

"But enough about my evening. What was up with you? You and Sean must have been on the dance floor for almost an hour straight."

"Chele, I don't know what's going on. But when Sean and I started working together on the latest marketing plan, something was different. We had a few late nights and a Saturday when we worked out of my home office. And we started talking about things besides work. We connected in a way that we hadn't done before. I didn't mean for that to happen; it just did."

"Mm-hmm. Have either of you said anything about this connection?"

"Not in so many words. I mean, there's this undercurrent when we're in the same room, but I think it would be a mistake to talk about it."

"Why?"

Michele had turned in her seat so she could look at me. I was glad I needed to keep my eyes on the road. "As long as neither of us says anything, we can pretend it's not real and nothing has to change. I won't feel like the sinner who's damned to hell and he'll still be considered a faithful husband. Once the words are out, one of us may feel obligated to move this to another level. And I'm not even sure what "this" is. I mean, we work together! I don't want people calling me a home wrecker. Especially when I think about what just happened to me. And what about my witness for God? It's bad enough Michael and I lived together for three years. I can't be known as an adulterer." Just the thought made me cringe.

"Correct me if I'm wrong, but you seem to be more concerned with what people at work would think than what God would think."

"I wish I could correct you, but the truth is, God is more forgiving than people. He would be disappointed in me, but at least He knows what I'm going through, and He would forgive me. The people at work wouldn't. I'm a Senior VP, soon to be partner, and I can't risk losing that for a fling. When you get right down to it, I'm only feeling all hot and bothered because Michael is gone."

"Is that the only reason?"

"It's the only reason I'm willing to acknowledge. If Michael was still around and acting right and still interested in what a woman has to offer, Sean wouldn't be a thought."

Michele pursed her lips. "Really?"

"You don't believe me?"

"Actually, I don't."

"Why?"

"Because you and Sean have always had chemistry. But after what went down with you and Michael, I think you opened yourself up to Sean. Especially since you and I both know you don't like to be alone."

My silence prompted her to continue. "There are a lot of qualities in Sean that you find attractive, but sweetie, he's married. And even if he were truly available to you, you still haven't given yourself time to heal. You were in a 12-year relationship with Michael. Practically married, but you never got the ring. You cooked, cleaned, and did everything a wife is expected to do. And you took care of him when he lost his job three years ago and never got another one. You let him move in with you and sponge off you. You saw potential in him, that didn't exist. And he repaid you by cheating on you. With a dude. Correct me if I'm wrong, but that's a pretty clear sign that there really wasn't ever a future for the two of you. Personally, I'm glad you didn't marry him and he's out of your life."

Everything she said was the truth. And it was a truth I didn't want talk about. But she kept on beating that darn dead horse. "I know you, Chanelle. I know that you are still hurting. And you're vulnerable. And not only do I know it, but let's go spiritual. The devil knows it too. Did he tempt Eve with a lemon? No. He got her with an apple. Something she liked. Sean's your apple."

I was so ready for this conversation to end. "Humph. Technically, the Bible didn't say it was an apple, but I hear ya. And you're right. About everything. Sean is a big red delicious apple, hand-picked only for me and I want to take a bite. A big bite. And even though I know better, just thinking about that apple makes my mouth water." I wished to God that what I was saying wasn't true. But it was.

"Hurry up and let's get your lusty butt to church. You need Jesus!"

"Don't we all?" We both laughed. I picked up Rachel and we headed to church to get the spiritual cleansing I so desperately needed.

Chapter 3

"Let the church say 'amen'," Pastor Sharpe commanded from the pulpit.

"Amen," the congregation responded.

"I said let the church say 'amen'!"

"Amen!"

"Thank you, Lord. You may be seated."

We took our seats and the servant of God began her morning message. "Good morning, Church."

"Good morning!"

"1 Corinthians 10:13 says 'No temptation has overtaken you except such as is common to man; but God is faithful, who will not allow you to be tempted beyond what you are able, but with the temptation will also make the way of escape, that you may be able to bear it'. Today, I want to talk to you about temptation. And not just any temptation, but lustful temptation."

"Ooh, Pastor, preach it!" someone in the back pew bellowed.

"There's a devil out there, Saints. And he wants your families. He wants your marriages. And you have to be strong. You have to resist the temptation."

"Yes," someone else shouted.

I struggled to sit still as the message began to hit very close to home. I kept my head glued to my Bible, afraid that if she caught my eye she'd know the thoughts I'd been having.

"When satan sets out to destroy you, he's gonna use something he knows you like. He's gonna wait until you are at your weakest point and then he's gonna STRIKE! But you have a weapon, Saints. And that weapon is Jesus!"

More agreement from the Amen corner and I just wanted everyone to be quiet so she could finish her message. But she took her time and spent a solid hour, quoting scripture after scripture, about the value of resisting temptation and that the wages of sin was death. This was the first Sunday in years that I wished I'd slept in and missed. After service, I stood in the meet and greet line and shook her hand, expecting her to give me the cursory, "Thank you for coming" handshake. But she didn't. Instead, she held my hand and then covered it with her other hand and looked me in my eyes. "Good morning, Sister Chanelle."

"Good morning, Reverend."

"How are you doing today?" she asked, knowing that God had told her I was struggling with my emotions.

"I'm fine."

"Are you sure about that?"

"Um, yes, yes, I'm sure."

"You know God loves you, right?" she asked, not blinking once as she stared straight through to the core of my soul.

"Of course."

"He's telling me to tell you, not to do it. Whatever it is you're contemplating, He said: It won't end well."

I stammered, "I, I don't know what you're talking about."

"I think you do. And I'm not asking you to tell me what's going on. But I'm here for you if you need me. And more importantly, God is here for you if you want to talk to Him about whatever it is you're dealing with."

"Uh, thank you, Pastor, but I'm fine."

I slowly slid my now damp hand from between hers.

"Be blessed, Sister Chanelle."

"You too, Pastor." I quickly walked away as she moved on to greet Rachel.

"Auntie, what was that all about?" Rachel asked me as we walked back to our vehicle.

"Uh, I'm not sure, Rach."

"She seemed to be warning you about something," Rachel persisted.

I was still shaken by my awkward conversation with my Pastor. I was not about to have a repeat with an 11-year old. "Let it go. I don't know what she was talking about. Now, do you want to grab something to eat before I take you home?"

My normally precocious niece would have stayed on me until I gave her an answer that satisfied her. But today, she cut me some slack. "Okay. Can we go to Chipotle?"

"You got it," I said, as we reached the Rover and got inside. We waited for Michele and BJ. Then the four of us headed to Rachel's favorite restaurant and I tried to pretend that I hadn't just received a warning directly from the Throne.

Chapter 4

Sitting at my office desk, I couldn't take my mind off Sunday. The conversation with Michele, the sermon, and most disturbingly, my interaction with Reverend Sharpe. She'd been my pastor since I was a little girl, so she knew me well. I'd fully expected to receive words of encouragement from her message, but instead, I got a holy beat down. Rev. Sharpe was on fire and her words, and her warning, pierced me to my core.

Last night as sleep eluded me, I resolved to keep my relationship with Sean strictly about business.

"Knock, knock." I looked up to see Sean standing at my office door. He looked scrumptious in a navy blue Armani suit with a matching winter coat thrown over his arm. I had to remind myself that my goal was to remain all business.

"Good morning." I gestured for him to come in and have a seat. "So, what brings you by?"

"I have a meeting with Mr. Jeffries and traffic was lighter than usual, so I got here early. As luck would have it, Mr. Jeffries had an emergency meeting, so he had to push our appointment to 11:00."

"Oh." I wasn't sure what else to say.

He asked about the rest of my weekend and we chatted for a few moments and then he said, "Since I have some time, I was going to Starbucks. Would you like to join me?"

Say no, say no, say no, I told myself. "Sure." We stood and walked over to my door. He was such a gentleman, as he helped me with my coat, then put on his own. He was so close to me, I could barely breathe. My business mindset was slowly slipping away. As we walked out, my assistant was coming in.

"Good morning, Boss Lady."

"Good morning, Patty. How was your evening?"

"The same as always. Kids fightin', husband whinin'. My bad ankle was actin' up and you know I have arthritis in my toes. And my..."

I cut her off. "I'm sorry to hear that, but I'm actually headed out." I hated to be rude, but Patty could go on and on about how tough life was. I sometimes started to dread my life listening to her talk about hers.

A few years ago, our company participated in a government pilot program where we hired women from abusive situations who were re-entering the workforce. Unfortunately, many of the women didn't work out, but Patty was one who made it. It was undeniable that she was unconventional, but she was an excellent assistant and I would put her up against any other assistant any time or day of the week. Listening to her problems and broken dialogue was a small price to pay for the value she added to my team. And surprisingly, she was very well received by my clients.

"Okay, well I'll see you when you get back."

"I'm going to Starbucks. Can I bring you anything?"

"Thanks, Boss Lady, but I'm good."

Once outside, Sean asked me if I wanted to drive to Starbucks.

"Nah, it's around the corner. I can use the exercise. Besides, it's a nice day." We each reached into our pockets and pulled out our gloves.

"So, tell me more about the project you're working on," Sean said, as we began walking.

"Well, you've seen most of it, so you know we're bidding to be the technology provider for the new stadium downtown. I have all the data collected. But I have to add a full-blown launch campaign and a few of my calculations aren't adding up. That's where I could use your help."

"We'll put our heads together and figure it out. Making you shine is my priority."

"Me?" I asked as I pointed to myself. I knew what he meant, but I decided to flirt a little.

He stuttered, "I mean, I mean, Jeffries Technology is my priority."

"What would it take to make me your priority? And I'm not talking about my company," I said, completely ignoring the warning I'd received yesterday.

"I would love to make you my priority. I didn't think you were interested."

"I shouldn't be." I hesitated. "I'm trying not to be." I hesitated again. "But I am." By now we were at the Starbucks counter and paused our conversation so we could place our order. Then, we sat down at a table for two in the corner.

"So, you were saying that you have an interest in me and you wish you didn't?" He prompted me to continue sharing feelings I'd never expected to tell him over my caramel macchiato.

"To be honest, I don't understand what I'm feeling about you or for you. What do you feel about me?" I wanted to know what was on his mind. As it was, I had already said too much. I chastised myself as I thought about how I should have never left my office.

"I'm a little mixed, too. I've never looked at another woman since I've been married. But every time I'm with you, I feel something that I never felt with Cynthia."

"And what's that?"

"A sense of security. I feel like I measure up when I'm with you. When we're working, you don't instantly criticize my ideas, even when they're outlandish. If you don't want to go with a concept I've designed, you make it into a joke. You take the sting out of your nos. I don't blame Cynthia for being who she is. I mean, she had it really rough growing up." He stopped himself and changed the subject. "Chanelle, we've had a lot of conversations that had nothing to do with work, right?"

I wasn't sure where he was going, but I nodded. "Yes, we have."

He took a deep breath and then continued. "I'm going to tell you some things about Cynthia. Not because I want you to judge my wife, but because I want you to understand a little more about what's been going on in my marriage. And why I'm feeling what I'm feeling about you."

I reached out to touch his hand. "Sean, you're my friend. You can tell me anything."

He looked down at our hands and then looked me in my eyes. "Cynthia used to drink heavily. To the point where she was an alcoholic. When I met her, she was in recovery and getting her life on track. As long as she attends her weekly AA meetings she's fine."

I shook my head. "That's good. But I'm still not following why you're sharing this with me."

"Because I want you to know," he paused. "Because I want you to know why I feel obligated to her."

"Sean, she's your wife. No explanation is needed."

"I feel it is. If I thought she'd be okay, I'd leave her."

"Whoa," I pulled back a little. "I'm not asking you to leave your spouse."

"I know. I'm just saying I would. I would leave her for you. That's how much I want to explore a relationship with you."

"Um…"

"I'm not looking for a response, so you don't have to figure out what to say." He took another deep breath, then continued. "Cynthia's been offered a job at one of the major pet hospitals in Virginia. And she has contacts out there with Handle Marketing. She wants me to set up an interview."

Now I understood why he was telling me all of this. He was contemplating leaving. "Handle Marketing? Aren't they your largest competitor?"

"Yeah. They're the biggest marketing consultant firm in the industry."

"Cynthia or no Cynthia, why wouldn't you jump at the chance to meet with them? This is a huge opportunity."

"I've been working at Image for six years and I enjoy it. And I like Michigan. Besides that, my family is here. I'm not psyched about the idea of moving to Virginia when Cynthia and I aren't even getting along that well. And then there's you. I'm not ready to leave you, Chanelle."

"Sean, you have to take me out of the equation and do what's best for *you*. I'm sure she wants you there with her."

He nodded. "She does. Since this whole thing started, she's been on me to make a decision; and she's been pointing out all the reasons why we need to move." He gave a long sigh before continuing. "But she's also been going on these so called on-call jobs late at night and staying gone for hours."

"Like at the party on Saturday?" I asked softly.

"Exactly. Her excuses don't make any sense, but I let her think I believe her."

"Do you think she's having an affair?" I continued to keep my voice soft so he would know that I was genuinely concerned.

"My pride would like me to believe she isn't, but I'm not stupid. If she hasn't yet, then it's in the process."

"How would you feel if that were true?" The conversation had evolved into something a lot deeper than I'd anticipated. We had gone from playful, if not reckless flirting, to a deep discussion about his marriage.

"I've given that lots of thought. Part of me would be relieved."

"Seriously?" I said, knitting my brows together. "You'd be relieved that your wife was cheating on you? That's doesn't make sense."

He nodded. "Yeah, I would. Because I wouldn't feel guilty about doing my own thing. But there's another part of me that would feel betrayed. I don't know which part would be greater."

"Are you still in love with her?"

"I do love her."

"That's not what I asked. Are you *in* love with your wife?"

"Yeah, I am."

Ugh! "Well, then that makes two things painfully obvious. The first is that no matter what you may feel for me, you owe it to your marriage to give it everything you have and try and make it work. Without the distraction of me, or some man that you're wife may be seeing."

He was thoughtful as he digested my words. "That's one. What's the other?"

"You need to go on that interview in Virginia. If it doesn't work out, I'm sure Mr. Jeffries and Image would take you back."

"You think so?"

"Yeah, I do. I'd be sorry to see you leave but you need to try. As long as you help me with my presentation before you go." I smiled to let him know we were still cool.

"I'd do anything for you. You are going to make some man happy one day."

I smacked my lips. "He'd better be ecstatic about being with me!"

We laughed and then he turned serious. "You know, Chanelle, I have a lot of respect for you. Not many women would do what you just did."

"I know. But right is right." And sometimes right was lonely, but I knew deep inside that I could never share some other woman's husband any more than I would share mine. Even if he was fine and had big…feet.

Chapter 5

"Counselor, where is your client?" the judge asked Rocco's attorney.

The judge had called us to our respective podiums and I was thankful that Michele had kept her word and come with me. I looked at my traitor of an ex, sitting on the hard bench on the plaintiff's side of the courtroom. He was looking back at the door, probably hoping his boy toy would walk through the doors with a good reason for being late. Late for a court case that he had instigated!

"Your Honor, I don't know," the man stealer's lawyer began. "He was supposed to meet me here this morning, but I haven't seen him. I sent him a text and I'm waiting on his response. I'm sure whatever has him delayed was unavoidable, as I know that he was anxious to have this issue resolved and have Ms. Slate pay the consequence of her careless and reckless actions."

"Counselor, if being on time for court isn't a priority for your client, then hearing his case is not a priority for me. Case dismissed." She banged her gavel.

I looked over at Michele, who was sitting just behind the wooden rail that separated the audience from the litigants.

"That's it?" she mouthed.

Having never stepped foot inside of a courtroom, not even for a traffic ticket, I shrugged and mouthed back, "I guess so."

Rocco's lawyer picked up his phone and began texting as he exited the courtroom. I was positive he was letting his loser of a client know that he'd just lost.

Michael and the attorney were standing in the hall when Michele and I walked out. The attorney glared at me as we passed and I met his glare with my own eye roll, glad that this mess was over. I never should have been sued in the first place, and if Rocco's kahunas never worked right again, it was his own fault.

As Michele and I approached the elevator, Michael called my name. I started not to turn around, but I surrendered to my curiosity and stopped in the middle of the hall and let him catch up.

"What do you want?"

"I want to apologize. I've given it some thought and I understand why you did what you did. I would have thrown me out too if I was you."

I studied my ex, trying to figure out his angle. "Thank you for the apology." I turned to continue toward the elevator, but he called me again.

"Chanelle, I miss talking to you everyday and I was wondering if you would be open to us rekindling our friendship?"

"Have you switched to a cheap brand of crack?"

"Huh?"

"You must be on the pipe. Because that is the only reason I can think of that would make you think we'd ever be friends again. After 12 years of being faithful to you, you repaid my faithfulness by cheating on me. And you didn't even have the decency to take it away from our home. And then you had the audacity to support that homewreckin' son of a biscuit eater when he chose to sue me. *Me!* So no, I have zero desire to be friends. This case is over and I'm moving on with my life. I suggest you do the same."

I turned and once again, headed toward the elevator. This time, he was wise enough not to stop me. But my luck didn't turn for the better, because when the elevator doors opened, Rocco stepped off, looking down at his cell phone.

Michele grabbed my arm. "Ignore him, Chanelle. Pretend you don't see him," she said, escorting me past Rocco and onto the elevator.

But he wouldn't allow me to ignore him, because he quickly spun around, putting his hand on the elevator door jam, preventing it from closing. "You only won because I got caught in traffic and couldn't get here on time."

"No, I won because your case was idiotic and you should have never come after me in the first place."

"I have to have surgery because of you."

"You have to have surgery because what goes around comes around. And karma bit you in the balls."

Michele gasped.

"Now, please move your hand before I force you to move it."

Rocco backed away, allowing the doors to finally close, but the last words I heard before we started our descent to the first floor were, "This isn't over, Missy!"

"Yeah, yeah," I muttered. Then looked at Michele. "Can you believe them?"

"I can't."

"And how could Michael think that he and I could ever be friends again? Ugh!"

"How about we grab a late breakfast so you can decompress?"

"Actually, I think I'll go in to the office. I still have a lot of work to do on my proposal," I said as we exited the elevator and walked outside.

"Are you talking about the one Sean is helping you with?"

"Yup."

"Have you seen him since you two went to Starbucks last week?"

"You mean, since I laid my feelings on the line? Only to find out that he's possibly moving? No, I haven't."

"Do you think he went on the interview?"

I nodded. "Of course. It's a great opportunity. And usually, I would have heard from him by now. We see each other a few times a week." We reached my car and I placed my hand on the handle, unlocking the door. "Thanks for being my support system today."

"No thanks needed. You'd do the same for me. I'm just glad it's all over."

"I hope it is. Although, Rocco sounds like he wants to keep it going." I hugged my best friend and got in my car. "I'll call you later."

"K. Love you."

"Love you, too."

"Boss Lady, Sean is on Line 1," Patty said through the phone intercom.

"Thanks, Patty. Please put him through."

Seconds later, I said, "Hey, stranger. Long time, no hear from."

"I know. It's been crazy busy. But, um, do you have time to meet me at Starbucks? I have something I'd like to share with you."

My heart fluttered just thinking about what he wanted to say. If it was work related, then we could talk now. "Sure. I can be there in about 30 minutes."

"Okay, I'll see you then."

After we hung up, I pulled out my cosmetic bag and freshened my makeup. I had no idea what he was going to tell me, but I was positive it was about the job in Virginia. Maybe he'd decided he wasn't going to interview and Cynthia was moving without him.

But that wasn't what he said. I sat across from him at "our" table, waiting to hear what was so important. And then he dropped a bombshell that left me unable to breathe.

"Chanelle, they hired me on the spot. I called them after you and I talked last Monday and they flew me out the next day. They loved me and I think this will be a very good move for me. And for my marriage. You were right. I have to do all I can to make it work with Cynthia."

My heart sank to the bottom of my feet. But I didn't want him to know that. I didn't want him to know that I was hoping for something more between us. So I took a deep breath and said, "I'm happy for you, Sean. You're doing the right thing. When do you leave?"

"Things are happening at lightning speed. The position I'm taking has been vacant for about five months and they're desperate. I start in two weeks."

I nodded and swallowed the ridiculously large lump in my throat. "Two weeks. Wow. That's fast."

He reached across the table, and caressed my hands. "I'll miss you, Chanelle. You're a good woman. You'll make some man very happy."

I hung my head slightly, not wanting him to see the tears that were threatening to give away my true feelings. "Humph. That's what you keep telling me."

"I say it because I mean it."

I inhaled deeply, held it for a few seconds, and then exhaled slowly. When I lifted my head, I looked him in the eyes and tried to lighten the mood. "Well, you promised to help me with my presentation. And I'm expecting you to keep your word." I gave a weak attempt at a smile.

He returned the smile. "I'm not leaving until it's perfect."

We stared at each other for a few moments and then went our separate ways. I had no idea where he went, but after the roller coaster of emotions I'd experienced in the last several hours, I went home.

Chapter 6

"Whatcha doin'?" I asked Michele when she picked up the phone.

"Nothing much. You know BJ is in the Saturday kid's basketball league at the youth center, so he and Ben are gone for most of the day.

"Wanna hit the mall? Macy's is having a 13-hour sale today."

"Of course, I want to go. You driving or riding?"

"Riding. I drove last time. Besides you have to pass right by my house to get to the mall."

"Okay. I'll see you in a couple of hours. I want to do a little housekeeping before I leave. Once we hit the street, there's no telling what time we'll be back."

"You're right about that. I need to do a little cleaning, too. How about you be here at 11:00?"

"Sounds like a plan. Just make sure you're ready!"

"I'm not the one who's slow. That would be you!"

She chuckled. "Guilty as charged. See you at 11."

As soon as we hung up, my phone rang. I glanced at the caller ID, and sighed. "Hello, Andrea." I said dryly to my sister knowing that if she called, it meant she wanted something.

"Don't sound so excited," Andrea said.

"Sorry. What's up?" Still cautious of her reasons for ringing me this early on a Saturday morning.

"Can't I call to check on my favorite baby sister?" Her voice was dripping with sugar. Whatever she wanted was going to be big.

"I'm your only sister."

"Yeah, yeah, yeah. Look, I'll get right to the point." There. That's the Andrea I was waiting to appear. "I'm 'bout to get evicted. I need you to let me hold a couple G's 'til I get paid."

"Two thousand dollars! Your rent is only $500."

"Well, I'm behind on some other bills and I figured since I was askin', I should throw in enough for my weave. It's a hot mess and I need it to be tight. Dante is takin' me to Vegas next weekend. You know I gots ta be fly."

Sometimes I really thought my sister was on some kind of very strong narcotic. "If Dante can afford to take you to Vegas, then why can't you get the money you need from him?"

"Uh, duh, if he pays for my bills, then how can he afford a Vegas vacation too?" my simpleminded sister asked.

"So, let me get this straight. You want me to pay for your necessities, including your weave?"

"Yeah."

"And in the meantime, instead of handling responsibilities, your man is paying for your trip?"

"Now, you feel me."

"Andrea, I don't know how to break this to you, but I am not giving it to you."

"Really? Why?"

I pulled the phone away from my ear and stared at it as though it was the irrational one, and not my sister. "Because you're a grown woman. Handle your own business."

"Well. How about $500 for my rent? Will you let me hold that?"

"Will I ever get it back?"

"Truth or lie?"

"Truth."

"No."

I shook my head and chuckled. When my sister and I were kids, we made a pact with each other. Anytime we said "truth or lie," we had to be 100% honest. And it worked. We never lied when we said "truth or lie." It was a strange sister code that we shared. "And you're probably going to bug me until I give in. Aren't you?"

"You know it."

"Fine. You can have the $500. When will you be by?"

"Well… how about now? Open ya door."

"Are you kidding me?" I exclaimed, as I stomped through my house and opened my front door. Sure enough, there was my sister. In a turtleneck, long sleeve minidress, thigh high boots, and a burgundy weave that easily went to her butt. I looked past her to the street and saw Dante behind the wheel of his much too big, and I'm sure close to being repossessed, SUV. I sighed. Hopefully, one day my sister would wake up and get her sorry act together.

"I knew you would say yes." Andrea grinned, flashing me a smile that reminded me that underneath her hoodrat exterior, she really was a beautiful woman.

I turned away from the door and headed to my office. Andrea followed. I took five 100 dollar bills from my petty cash box and handed them to her. "You know this is ridiculous, don't you? You should have money."

"I got caught in a mess with those cash advance places. I'm in to them for a lot of money."

"Well, I'm not bailing you out of that mess like I did last time."

Andrea gave me a devilish smirk as she waved the $500 I had just given her in my face. "You just did, lil' sis," she said as she began backing out of the room. She quickly added, "But I promise, this is the last time I get caught up wit all dat. Love you." I made a move toward her, but she grabbed my shoulders and kissed me on my cheek. Then she spun on her heels and darted through my house and out the door, leaving me $500 poorer and speechless.

I sat on my couch and stared out the window lost in my thoughts. I had gone from murderous thoughts toward my sister to more wistful thoughts of Sean. He'd given his two weeks' notice to Mr. Jeffries and this coming Friday was going to be his last day. He kept his word though, about my presentation. He'd taken it home yesterday to review my final draft and told me he'd give it back on Monday. I was anxious to hear what he had to say about it, because I was due to give a dry run to Mr. Jeffries on Tuesday and present it to my client on Thursday.

I glanced at the clock on the living room wall. It was only 9:43. I had plenty of time before Michele arrived. I had already done my Pilates, showered, and was lounging in my favorite orange sarong that doubled as a robe. I turned my attention from blankly staring outside and switched on the television. Lifetime was having a Golden Girls marathon and I loved those old ladies.

It was a bitterly cold and snowy day and I was no longer in the mood for shopping.

I picked up the phone to call Michele and tell her I'd changed my mind, but before I could dial her number my doorbell rang.

"It better not be Andrea coming back for more," I mumbled, marching to the door. I looked through the peephole and felt my stomach flip.

I put my hand to my hair and realized I still had on my scarf. I snatched it off and gave a quick shake to my head to let my curls fall to my shoulders. I smoothed my sarong to make sure it was closed, and then greeted my guest.

"Good morning!" I flashed Sean my brightest smile. "What brings you by?"

"I was in the neighborhood and decided to bring you your proposal. I would have called first, but I left my phone at home. I hope you don't mind that I stopped by unannounced."

"I don't mind. Please come in." I stepped aside and allowed him to enter. I couldn't stop myself from staring at him. As he walked by, I inhaled deeply and took in the smell of his Jean Paul cologne. I bit my lower lip and closed the door.

He turned around to face me and I was captivated by his eyes. They were light brown with flecks of green and they seemed to dance when he smiled.

"Chanelle?" He had a puzzled look on his face.

"Huh?"

"So, where do you want to do it?"

"Anywhere you like," I answered breathlessly.

"Since it's your house, I'll let you decide."

"Decide what?"

"Where do you want to go over the proposal? I asked where you wanted to spread out. There were a couple of areas that I thought you could tighten up and I wanted to show you. Overall, I think it's a winner."

I snapped out of my daze. "Oh. Ah, yeah, right. Ummm, the proposal. Riiigghht. Um, how about here?" I pointed to the living room. "We can spread out on the coffee table and you show me what you're talking about."

I led him into the living room. "Make yourself comfortable. I'm going to change. I'll be right back," I said as I bounded up the steps to my bedroom. I scolded myself for acting like a star struck teen. Once inside, I closed the door and then leaned against it. I took several deep breaths in a useless attempt to try and calm my nerves.

How long had he been talking to me while I stared at him? Why did this man have such an effect on me? It was ridiculous.

I walked over to my bathroom and turned on the faucet. I hoped that splashing cold water on my face would help. It didn't. I turned off the water and headed to my closet. What could I throw on that said sexy casual? Did I even want to be sexy? Well, I knew I did, but I shouldn't. In the end, I threw on some navy sweats, a fitted yellow t-shirt, and white ankle socks. I said a quick prayer to God and then headed back downstairs.

Chapter 7

We reviewed every single page of the proposal. His suggestions were on point and I made notations to make the necessary changes. I was fully confident that by Thursday I would be more than prepared to land this account.

Michele had called around 10:30 and said she didn't feel like going out either. She was taking advantage of her afternoon home alone.

"Wow, I can't believe it's noon already!" Sean said as he stood up, raised his arms, and gave a big stretch.

"I know. Time flies when you're having fun." I grinned at him. I put my hands on the back of my neck and gave myself a light massage.

"Here, why don't you let me do that for you?" he offered.

I looked up at him. "That's okay. I'm just a little stiff from bending over those projections for so long." I rotated my neck as I continued to try to work out the kinks.

"I insist. I've been told that my hands are famous." He wiggled his fingers and gave me a goofy grin. There was no way that I could not give in.

I consented, "Alright."

"Turn your back to me."

I did as I was instructed and he stood behind me. I turned to mush the instant he touched me. As he rubbed my shoulders, I let my neck drop, enjoying the tingling sensation of his hands on my skin.

I closed my eyes and let my mind wander. It felt so good that I let out a low moan. He must have taken that as an invitation, because the next thing I knew his lips were on my neck. They were soft and warm. I ignored the four alarm fire blares that were going off in my head. I didn't want to do the rational, sensible thing. I wanted to give into the moment and deal with the consequences later.

I tilted my head so he would have better access to my neck, then I wrapped my hand around the back of his head and played with his hair. He touched my face and slowly he turned me around until we were staring into each other's eyes. I glanced down for a moment and was thankful that he wasn't wearing his wedding band. Not that it made him any less married; it just made it easier to pretend that what I was about to do was okay.

For a split second, I came to my senses and grabbed his hands before they went any further, but then he whispered, "Please" in my ear and his hot breath broke down every single one of my defenses.

We explored each other's bodies as we rid ourselves of all clothing. "Do you want to go to your room?" he asked, as he hovered over me.

"No, I want you right here. Right now." I stared at him and waited with anticipation.

We paused while he reached into his pants pockets, which were now on the floor, and pulled out a condom. He must have planned this before he got here. I didn't know if I should be grateful for the protection or pissed that he assumed it would go this far.

But as he entered me seconds later, I decided I was glad because I found myself floating to the most magical place I had ever been in my life and I didn't want to ever leave.

What in the hell did I do? I held my head in my hands, as I stood under the hot shower.

"Do you want some company?" he yelled from the other side of the bathroom door.

"Uh, no thank you," I stuttered. "I'll be out in a minute."

"Okay. Well, let me know if you change your mind."

"Thanks for the offer," I muttered.

I could not believe that we'd had sex all afternoon and then slept until late evening. I had never before in all my life been intimate with a man who wasn't mine. I was the one in my group of friends who didn't understand how other women did it. I was even judgmental of them.

Life had a cruel way of turning on you. I could hear Michele's mouth when I told her. And I was going to tell her because we talked about everything.

I briefly thought about Michael and blamed him. If he had been who I needed him to be, we would've been married, and this wouldn't have been an issue.

Yeah, right, Chanelle, who are you kidding? I chastised myself. It wasn't Michael's fault. An opportunity had presented itself, and I took it. I probably shouldn't have. I know I shouldn't have.

But I did. And I loved it. I wished it could happen again. But it couldn't. For one, he was moving at the end of the week. For two, my conscience wouldn't allow a repeat. Now I had to figure out a way to get him out of my house.

After my shower, I put on my flannel pajamas, the most unflattering thing I owned. The last thing I wanted was to walk out of the bathroom looking enticing.

My heart was racing. What if he expected us to pick up where we left off? Would I have the strength to say no or would I do it again? Whether I remained strong or crumbled, I couldn't hide in my bathroom all night.

I slowly opened the door and walked out. He was sitting on the side of my bed with his head in his hands. He looked up when he heard me and his eyes were red.

"Hi."

"Hi."

"I'm really sorry, Chanelle. I don't know what happened. I mean I know what happened, I'm just sorry that it did. I mean, I'm not sorry, but I am. You know what I'm tryin' to say?"

He was as tormented by this as I was. He should have been even more so because he was the one who was married. "I think I know. I feel bad about this, too." I sat next to him and reached for his hand. I took a deep breath. "Sometimes things just have a way of spinning out of control."

"Yeah, they do, but I wanted this to happen. That's why I came over. I could have given you the proposal on Monday. I just wanted to spend some time alone with you."

"I know. I'm not slow, Sean. Don't think that you seduced me and I didn't know what was up. I wanted to do this as much as you did. You're a good friend and I value our relationship. I'm not going to say anything about this to anyone. Are you?"

"If you mean am I going to tell my wife, the answer is no. We have enough issues to work through. But I would be lying to you, Chanelle, if I said I didn't feel something when I'm with you that I don't feel with her."

My heart was so sad. I'd spent a loving and sensual afternoon with a man I cared about and there was no future for us. "I understand. But you're doing the right thing. You have to give your marriage a chance. Virginia will be a good start for both of you."

He squeezed my hand. "I'm going to miss you."

"I'm going to miss you, too."

He stood up and gave me a half smile. "I guess I should head home. I need to figure out how I am going to explain my day."

"Good luck."

I walked him to the front door. I wanted to kiss him before he left, but I was afraid that I wouldn't be able to handle it. Instead, I allowed him to pull me close and hold me like I was his woman. I closed my eyes and inhaled, breathing in the moment knowing that in seconds all I would have were memories of what once was, but could never really be. I finally peeled myself away from his embrace and with watery eyes, I stood at the door and watched him walk to his car and drive away. I slowly closed the door and dragged myself back to my bedroom. What a day!

Chapter 8

I reached my hand from underneath my blanket and grabbed the phone. "Hey, Michele," I said when she answered. "Ride with me to church, okay?"

"O-K. Is everything alright?"

"Yeah," I replied in a low tone. "I just need my best friend."

"I'll be ready when you get here."

We disconnected the call and I placed my hands over my eyes and groaned. I'd had a tumultuous night, tossing and turning and tossing and turning. I finally dragged myself from my bed, skipped my workout, and fixed a jumbo cup of coffee.

"You are such a hypocrite," I said aloud, talking to myself as though I belonged in a psych ward. "Here you are, getting ready for church. Getting ready to praise the Lord." I raised my hands and twisted them from side to side. "And you just did 'the do' with another woman's husband. Ugh." I was so disgusted with myself.

Stepping into my bathroom, I cringed. The dated décor of the place that was supposed to bring me serenity was actually worsening my already sour mood. The former owners had some love affair with pink and tiny tiled floors with grout that was impossible to clean. I'd dealt with it for much too long and I was going to have to make a change soon.

It took me longer than usual to prepare and by the time I got to Michele's, we were already late. "What happened to Miss Always On Time?" she joked, getting into the car and closing the door.

"I had a rough morning."

She took a good look at me. "Wow. I can see that. What happened?"

"Let's go to Red Lobster after church and I'll fill you in."

Michele gave me the side-eye as she tried to figure out what was up. "Okay. Okay. Sooo... what do you want to talk about now?"

"Nothing. I just want to ride in silence."

"Let me get this straight. You wanted me to ride with you, so we could *not* talk?"

I nodded. "Yes."

Then she nodded. "Okay."

That's the beauty of having a best friend. They understand you in ways that no one else will. We drove in silence and had an uneventful time in church, although, I was totally convicted. The sermon message was "Let Your Actions Support Your Words". Humph, my actions these days were a long way from what I professed. But I made it through the morning, dodged Pastor Sharpe at the after service meet and greet, and now we were seated at Red Lobster and had placed our orders.

"What's going on?" she asked, before taking a sip of her hot tea.

"Sean and I had sex all day yesterday," I blurted.

She paused with her cup in mid-air. "Come again?"

"I did. And again and again and again."

"Whoa. How did *that* happen?"

I filled her in on the details of the day before, starting with him knocking on my door and ending with him leaving hours later.

"Wow... How do you feel about all of this?"

I shrugged. "Guilty. Sad. Like I just lost a good friend. Like the worst Christian ever."

Michele was silent and I kept talking. "It never should have happened, Chele. I knew better."

"Yeah, you did," she said, and I rolled my eyes. "Am I lying?"

I shook my head. "No."

"But, hey, what's done is done. Lamenting about it doesn't change it."

"But you remember what Pastor Sharpe said to me a few weeks ago, right?"

"You mean, the warning about whatever you were planning to do, don't do it? Because it won't end well?"

"That's exactly what I'm talking about. This has to be what she was talking about."

Michele pondered what I said and then asked, "The only question now is, what are you gonna do?"

I took a bite of the cheddar biscuits that had been placed on our table and shrugged again. "The only thing I can do. Keep it moving. I asked God to forgive me, and I know He did. Eventually, I'll forgive myself. Sean will be gone at the end of the week, and I'll get my focus back."

Michele nodded while she scooped some of the lobster artichoke dip onto a chip and shoveled the entire thing into her mouth. She held up her finger, while she finished chewing, then said, "You'll be fine, girl. You just have to take some time for yourself. Get your head right."

"Yeah, and pray that karma doesn't get me too bad. God says we reap what we sow. And this is a messed up crop I just planted."

"It is. But it's not the end of the world. You'll bounce back from this."

"Lord knows I hope so," I said, falling into the plush leather seat of the booth and blowing the air out of my cheeks. "Lord knows I hope so."

Chapter 9

"Hey, Chanelle," Sean said when he phoned me in my office the Wednesday following our tryst.

"Hey."

"Would you mind meeting me at Starbucks in about an hour?"

Good Lord! I was starting to hate Starbucks. "Is it something we can talk about here? Maybe before your going away party?" Mr. Jeffries had arranged a final farewell for Sean around 3:00.

"Um, I was hoping to see you alone."

"Why?"

"Because what I need to say can't be said in the office."

I wondered what God-awful news he was going to drop on me now, but after a moment of hesitation, I said, "Sure. I can be there in an hour."

"Thanks. See you then."

"Yeah, yeah." I hung up and tilted forward, placing my elbows on my desk and my head in my palms.

"Thank you for meeting me," he said, standing as I approached the table.

"You're welcome." I allowed him to kiss my cheek, before both of us sat down.

"I ordered your favorite, a caramel macchiato," he said, pointing to the steaming hot drink in front of me.

"Thanks. I didn't realize you noticed what I drink."

"I notice a lot of things about you."

Why was this man doing this to me? "So, what did you want to talk about?" I asked, getting down to business and trying to pretend that my heart wasn't being torn to shreds.

He reached for my hands. "I just wanted to make sure you were okay. After what happened on Saturday."

"Why wouldn't I be okay? We both knew what was up," I said, sliding my hands back and placing them in my lap, underneath the table.

"Chanelle, I want to apologize to you again. I never should have let it happen."

"Look, Sean. We've already had this conversation. I said we're good. If this is all you wanted to say, then you could have saved your breath." I made a move to stand, but he leaned forward and touched my arm.

"Please, don't leave. Not yet. Please." His eyes pleaded with me to stay put, and against my better judgment, I sat back down. He exhaled. "Thank you. The reason I asked you to meet me was because I wanted to give you this." Reaching into his pocket, he pulled out a small jewelry box, then slid it across the table and next to my macchiato.

I stared at it like I'd be electrocuted if I touched it. "What is it?"

"Open it and see," he prompted.

Did I really want a gift from him? Yes. No. Yes. Shoot, I dunno. I moaned inwardly, then opened the box. Inside was a two-carat diamond and platinum tennis bracelet. I held it in my hands, fingering the jewels. "Sean, this is beautiful," I whispered.

"I'm glad you like it."

"I love it," I said. "But I can't keep it." I handed it to him, but he wouldn't take it.

"Why?"

"Because it wouldn't be right. You're married."

"I told you, I really care about you. My situation is my situation. But I want you to know you'll always be in my heart. Please. Keep it." He slowly took it from my hand and fastened it around my wrist.

I was staring at it and wondering if I should remove it when a woman walked up to our booth.

"Hi, Sean," she cooed.

"Oh, uh, hi, Bianca," he said. Tiny beads of sweat instantly formed on his forehead.

"So, who's your little friend?" she asked, crossing her arms in front of her flat chest and cutting her eyes at me.

"Um, this is -," he began, but I interrupted him.

I removed the bracelet. "No need for names. I was just leaving." I slid out of the booth and exited the restaurant. This was without a doubt the last time I would ever step foot inside of a Starbucks!

"You're kidding me!" Michele said, when I'd called her as soon as I got back to my office.

"I wish. She walked right up to us and stared me down like I was trying to take her man or something."

The call waiting tone chimed for the fifth time since I'd left Sean. I didn't need to look at the number to know who it was.

"I didn't expect that from him," she said, commiserating with me.

I shook my head, ignoring the beep. "I didn't either. And here's what's messed up. He's not mine. So, technically, I can't even be upset. I thought I was special. The exception. But nope, I was just a side chick, probably in a long line of side chicks."

"Well, at least now you know."

"Yeah, but his going away party starts in less than 25 minutes. How am I supposed to act normal when I'm so angry? And hurt."

"You fake it. You can't be the jilted woman at work."

I breathed loudly. "You're right. This is my bread and butter. Look, I'll call you later. I need a few minutes to get my head right before I go into this party."

Immediately after we hung up, Mr. Jeffries knocked on my door. "Hey, Chanelle, did I catch you at a bad time?"

"Of course not," I said, waving him into my office.

He sat in the cushy seat in front of my mahogany desk. "I wanted to compliment you again for the work you did on your presentation. I believe we'll land the account tomorrow."

"Thank you. I'm confident things will go well."

"Sean helped you, right?"

I twisted in my seat, just a little. "Yes. Yes, he helped me."

"I'm going to miss him. He was a big asset around here."

I swallowed hard. "Yes. Yes, he was."

Mr. Jeffries was oblivious to my discomfort and kept talking. "I was thinking it might be a good idea for you to say a few words. You probably worked with him more than anyone else around here."

"Uh," I began, my eyes larger than a coaster for a cup, "uh, I, I think that's a great idea." I cleared my throat and continued. "I – I'd be happy to say a few words."

"Good. Good," he said, standing. "I need to make a quick call, but I'll see you in a few."

I nodded. "Yes, Mr. Jeffries."

As he was walking out, Sean was approaching my open door. "Well, if it isn't the man of the hour," the older gentleman said, slapping him on the arm, like a father proud of his son, and then, he kept going.

"Hello, Sir," Sean said to his retreating back, before entering my office. He was lucky. If Mr. Jeffries had been just a few steps further away, I would have slammed the door in his face.

"Hey," he said, closing my door, and coming toward me. But he froze in mid-step when he saw the daggers coming from my eyes.

"What do you want, Sean?"

"I just want to explain what that was back there."

"No need for explanations. I'm not your wife."

"Chanelle, please listen. Bianca means nothing to me and I'd forgotten all about her. She's just a woman I met a couple months ago when I was having a lonely moment, and she was company for the evening."

"You paid for sex?" I asked, curling my lip. "That's nasty."

"No, I didn't. I actually met her in a bar. It was a one-night thing. That's it."

I stood. "That's still nasty."

He ignored my comment, and continued. "Like I said, it was one-night that she wanted to be more. And she pops up from time to time. Like she has my schedule or something. But what am I gonna do? Report her?"

"So you're saying she's following you? This must be the day, I wore my dumb clothes." I walked toward the door, brushing past him, but he caught my arm.

"I didn't lie to you. My feelings for you are too deep for me to lie to you."

I looked down to where his hand was holding me and then looked into his eyes. Our faces were so close, I could feel his breath even though his mouth was closed. "Sean."

"Chanelle," he whispered my name and every ounce of resistance I'd had was washed away in a flood of lust. Then with his other hand, he cupped my chin and bent down to kiss me.

I was thankful that my office was on the 14th floor and there were no interior windows, because his kisses grew forceful as he backed me against the wall. When his lips moved down to my neck, he unzipped his pants then hiked up my skirt and pushed aside the only barrier between us. The next 20 minutes were explosive, both of us surrendering to the passion that gripped us and refused to let go.

Somehow, we pulled it together in time to walk into his party at 3:00 on the dot. I made it through my little speech, though I was clueless about what I'd said, since my mind kept replaying what had just happened. And I was still feeling a little tingly. But whatever I said must have been okay, because I got a few laughs and applause.

I mingled for a moment, then slipped out when no one was looking and went back to my office to grab my belongings. I was ready to go home and sort out this wild day.

When I entered my office, a sparkle on my desk peeked out from underneath a piece of paper. I walked over and realized Sean had left the diamond tennis bracelet and a note. *"Chanelle, thank you for being a wonderful woman. I would never hurt you. I love you."*

The note wasn't signed, but it didn't need to be. I fastened the gems around my wrist and sighed. The sooner this man moved, the simpler my life was going to be.

Chapter 10

"You need to get out and start dating. Sean has been gone for what, 3 weeks?" Michele said, over a cup of coffee at the now infamous Starbucks, that I'd sworn to myself I'd never enter again.

"Yeah, yeah, yeah. I'll get out in my own time," I said, absently stirring my coffee.

"If I set you up on a blind date, would you go?"

I turned up my nose. "I don't know about that."

"It would be with one of Ben's friend's. And you know he's got good friends. I wouldn't set you up with a loser."

"Hmm... Let me think about it."

"Well, well, well. Look who we have here," a familiar voice said.

Michele and I turned toward the sound. It was Sean's one-night stand.

"What do you want with me?" I asked her as she walked up to our table.

"It ain't you, honey. It's Sean. I'm letting you know right now. Stay away from him."

I screwed up my face. "What are you talking about? One, I don't know you, so you need to back up. And two, he's a colleague. A colleague who doesn't even live here anymore."

"Humph. Like I said. Stay away from him," she said.

"You have one more time to walk up on me and it's gonna be on and poppin'," I said to her, summoning my inner Andrea, and forgetting momentarily that I was a professional woman.

"Chick, I'm like the Incredible Hulk. Don't make me angry. You wouldn't like me when I'm angry."

"Who says unintelligent stuff like that? But if you're feeling froggy, then jump." I stood and opened my arms wide, inviting her to come at me.

But Michele also stood and placed her hands in front of me to block me from potentially swinging. "Chanelle, no. This is not who you are," she said, then turned to the woman who was about to receive a beating. "For your safety, you really need to leave."

The woman paused. "This ain't over. Believe that," she said.

"Pick the place and time. I'll be there," I said to her, retreating back.

Returning to our seats and pretending that patrons weren't staring at us, Michele said, "You've never had a fight in your life. What in the heck was *that* all about?"

"Girl, I have no idea, but that's the heifer I was telling you about. She's the one who walked up on Sean and me the last time we were here. Seeing her again just set me off."

"You are not a housewife on one of those reality shows. Pull it together."

I held up my hands. "You're right. I lost my cool for a second. But I'm back to normal now."

"Good. So why is she acting like Sean is your man?"

"How am I supposed to know? This is the second time I've ever seen her in my life." I shook my head, trying to erase the strange interaction that had just occurred.

"And did you really say 'if you're feeling froggy, then jump'?" She laughed.

I laughed with her. "You know I think I'm gangsta. Anyway," I said, checking my watch, "I have a meeting in 20 minutes, so I need to get back. I'll call you later."

"K. I'm going to finish my coffee and run some errands and pretend I didn't just see what I know I just saw."

"Right. And I'll pretend I didn't just do what I know I just did." I stood and bent down, kissing her on the cheek. Then went back to work.

Mr. Jeffries was going on and on about who knows what. But sitting in this meeting was torture. I was slightly rattled by my interaction with that woman at Starbucks and my over the top response. Why did she think Sean and I were a couple? And why did she even remember me? And why was I so ready to fight her? I doodled in my notebook, as though I were taking notes from the meeting, and prayed like a kid in class who didn't do her homework, that Mr. Jeffries wouldn't ask me any questions.

Finally, the meeting concluded, I said my goodbyes, packed up my laptop and went home.

Pulling into my driveway and waiting for the garage door to lift, gave me a sense of comfort, and I exhaled loudly as the tension of the day left my body. I entered the kitchen through the side door of the garage, tossed my keys on the counter and kicked off my shoes. I grabbed an ice cold beer from the fridge, selected a bland pre-packaged dinner from the freezer and popped it into the microwave. Then I headed upstairs to my bedroom to change into my favorite beat up sweats.

Coming back down the steps, I made a pit stop at the front door to grab the mail that had been slipped through the slot. I threw it on top of the pile that had been accumulating for the past 3 weeks and went back into the kitchen. Four minutes later, my meal, if I could even call it that, was cooked and I took it and my beer into the den, where I fully intended to be parked for the remainder of the evening.

I washed down what was supposed to be a piece of chicken with a swig of my frothy beverage and flipped through the cable channels, looking for mindless entertainment. When my phone rang, I almost ignored it, but then thought it might be important.

I answered, without bothering to check the caller ID.

"Hey, Chanelle, how's it going?" Sean asked.

My heart froze as I sat up straight on the couch. "Hey. Things are going well."

"I hope you don't mind me calling. I tried calling you before I left, but you wouldn't answer."

Of course I didn't answer, I thought. "I didn't see the point."

He cleared his throat. "Um, did you win the account?"

"Yes. Thank you for your help."

"Congratulations and you're welcome."

We listened to the sound of each other breathing as we struggled to hold an awkward conversation. "How's the new home?" I finally asked.

"Virginia is beautiful... I love the weather... My new job is good... Challenging, but good."

"Oh," I said. More silence as both of us danced around what I wanted to know, but was afraid to ask.

"Cynthia and I aren't doing so well," he volunteered.

"Oh. Um, sorry to hear that," I lied.

"Yeah, I thought the change of scenery would be good for us, but things seem to be getting worse." He paused. "I miss you, Chanelle. I miss working with you and seeing you almost everyday."

I didn't know how to respond. I missed him too, but I wasn't going to say it. It wasn't like we dated. "Well, hopefully, things will get better. Look, I'd love to talk more, but I have to go. I wish you all the best."

"Oh, okay," he said, surprised I was rushing him off the phone. "Well, I guess I'll talk to you later."

"Actually, Sean. I don't think that's such a good idea. We should have a clean break. You are building your life there and I'm living my life here."

"I'm not ready to let you go."

"You have no choice. I was never built to be a sidepiece. I made a mistake. A couple mistakes. And now I'm moving on. I suggest you do the same."

"Wow, I didn't expect this."

"I'm sure you didn't. As much as I care about you Sean, and I do, I really really care about you. But I care about myself more. You have a wife and a life that is separate from me. I'm not going to sit around and be the clean up woman, taking whatever I can get. I'm worth more than that. Don't you agree?" I put him on the spot, but I needed him to acknowledge that playing with my feelings was not cool.

"Yes, Chanelle, you are worth so much more."

"Thank you for that. Please don't call me again. Goodbye Sean," I said, and clicked the "off" button. Then I immediately turned the phone back on and dialed a familiar number.

"Hey, Chele, I think I'm ready for that date."

Chapter 11

"Michele, I hope you did right by me," I said aloud, walking into J. Alexander's for my first-ever blind date.

She was excited that I was willing to give it a try and set me up with Lawrence, the brother of one of Ben's closest friends. She said I'd met him before, though I couldn't remember him. Ben had given him my phone number and when he called me, I thought he was silly. But I chalked it up to nerves and decided to give him a chance anyway.

He was already there when I arrived. The waiter escorted me to the table and Lawrence stood when he saw me approach. One thing I could say about him was that he was definitely handsome! He had smooth chocolate skin, broad shoulders, and a body that would make a body builder jealous. Though, it was a little hard to get past the short s-curl he was sporting and the electric blue and cream pinstriped suit. I glanced at his feet and noticed he had on matching blue and cream gators. The smile he saw on my face as I greeted him was masking my laughter. This was going to be an interesting night, I thought.

"Hey, Chanelle." He leaned forward to kiss my cheek and I didn't want his lips on me. So I extended my hand. I was grateful that he got the message and didn't press the issue.

"Hi, Lawrence, how are you?" I continued to stand, as he pulled back my chair and allowed me to sit down before pushing it back toward the table.

"I'm fine, Baby. You look incredible. It's like you knew what I was going to wear," he slurred as he sat across from me.

It was true, I was looking good in my cream knit dress and matching boots, but I was not trying to be color coordinated with him and I was certainly not his baby. The last thing I wanted was for someone to think we knew each other that well. I was pretty sure that this would be a one-date night.

"So, what do you recommend?" he inquired, looking me up and down.

Feeling uncomfortable, I shifted in my seat and did my best to remain cordial. "Well, I love the grilled salmon, mashed potatoes, and their house salad. I order it every time I come."

"I like the way you say that. 'Every time I come.' Yeah, I like that." He gave me a lazy grin.

I couldn't believe Super Fly said that. And why was I just noticing that gold tooth?

"So, have you been here before?" I asked, changing the subject.

"Naw, this is my first time. But hopefully it won't be my last."

There he goes with that idiotic grin again, I thought. I offered, "I was hooked after my first time."

"I hope you get hooked after yo' first time wit me."

I was reaching my limit. "Don't you think it's a little soon to start thinking about a 'first time'?"

"It ain't never too soon. It's like this, Chanelle. This is a nice restaurant and I expect to be repaid."

This fool was out of his mind! "And just how do you expect me to repay you?"

He let his eyes drop to my generous cleavage and then back up to my face. "I think you know the answer to that question."

I paused briefly while I debated taking the classy road or cussin' him out. But I never had a chance to actually respond because out of nowhere a shrieking female voice said, "Ah ha! I knew I'd find you here with some sleazy trick bag."

We both turned to see an enraged and very pregnant woman barreling down on our table.

"Hey, Baby," he began, throwing up his hands to fend off her swinging fists.

"Don't you baby me," she screamed. "Here I am, 'bout ready to have yo' baby and you sittin' here with some chick. Buyin' her a dinner you won't even buy me!"

I looked from Lawrence to his wife or girlfriend or at the very least his baby mama, while he said, "Baby, it ain't like that. She my cousin."

"Uh uh. You done this for the last time." Then she turned her rage on me. "Look. I been with this man for 7 years. You hear me? 7 years! And I ain't about to give him up. If I ever catch you with my man again, you ain't gon' like what I do to you."

Had I just stepped into the ghetto edition of the Twilight Zone? "Um, you don't have to worry about me and your man. I promise you, I don't want him," I said, standing and smoothing the front of my dress.

"If you ain't want him, then why you havin' dinner with him, huh?"

Instead of going into details and delaying my exit from this nightmare, I said, "It was just a mistake. You have a good evening."

"Look here, you man stealing hussy. If I catch you with my dude again, I'll cut yo skinny little—"

I had a pretty good idea how she ended her sentence, but I missed it because I was already on the other side of the restaurant doors and practically sprinting to my car.

Once inside, I instructed my Bluetooth system to dial Michele's number. "Hello?"

"You are soooooooo on my list. You are going to have to kiss up to me for a long time before I forgive you for this one."

She feigned offense. "My, my, such hostility! And from such a sweet, demure young lady. I take it your date didn't go well?"

"Considering it started five minutes ago and I'm back in my car, you take it right. Why didn't you screen him?"

"I did screen him. Leonard is a very nice guy. What happened?"

"Who in the world is Leonard? I had a date with Lawrence." Now I was confused.

"Lawrence?" She said his name a couple of times and then all of a sudden I heard uncontrollable laughter.

"What's so funny?" I was steaming at the fact that she found anything humorous about my train wreck of a date.

"Ben must have given your number to the wrong brother. I am so sorry! Lawrence is a jerk."

"Tell me something I don't know! And this is not funny!" I was practically screaming in my car.

"Yeah, right. You know this is hilarious and if it had happened to anyone else you would be laughing, too." She snickered.

As she continued laughing, my frustration subsided and I saw the humor that had tickled her. We laughed while I described the events of the evening, including his outfit, gold tooth, S-curl, and girlfriend who looked like she should've given birth five months ago. I had to pull over because I was chuckling so hard I couldn't see the road. To appease me, she told me to come over and she would buy me a pizza. I told her to have it delivered to my home because if I saw Ben tonight, I was liable to choke him.

She completely understood and I arrived at home only moments before my pizza was delivered. I stopped by the kitchen and grabbed a beer, then took my drink and the entire pizza box to my bedroom. I quickly changed into my 'I'm home alone so it's okay to have this on' pajamas and got in the bed with my food and my drink, turned on the TV, and had a great Friday night.

And this was my first date post Sean? Ugh…Ay yi yi.

Chapter 12

7 Months Later

Good morning, Patty," I said to my assistant as I entered my office suite.

"Good morning, Boss Lady. How was ya night?"

"Same as usual, but it was alright. How was yours?"

"Fine. But are you sure about that, Boss Lady? You been lookin' a little tired these days. You sure everything is alright?"

Leave it to Patty to call me out. "I'm fine. Please hold my calls this morning. I have a couple things I need to get out by noon."

"You got it, Boss Lady."

I entered my office, placed my briefcase on the floor, then powered up my computer, following my usual routine.

My mouth dropped when I opened my email and the first message that popped up was from Michael. *"Hey, Chanelle, I know it's been awhile since we last spoke. I've been thinking about you a lot over the past several months. I'm emailing you because I figured you wouldn't accept my call. I'm genuinely sorry about what happened with Rocco. I was just confused at the time and things with him aren't what I expected. I think maybe I made a mistake. I know you weren't interested in remaining friends when we were at the courthouse, but months have passed and I'm hoping you'll reconsider. I'd love it if we could have drinks one day after you get off work. I'd like to talk about us."*

Wow. I sat back in my executive chair and stared at the computer monitor, re-reading the words over and over. I hadn't expected to ever hear from him again and I wondered how I should respond. Or *if* I should respond.

I spun in my chair and gazed out the window at the skyline. The last seven months had been very lonely. Many nights of frozen dinners and mindless TV. A couple of pitiful dates, just as bad as the one with Lawrence, who by the way I'd actually run into at the gas station and we'd briefly talked. Until his off-her-meds baby mama came charging out of the store connected to the station and started yelling at me to stay away from her man. Like I'd want Mr. Gold Tooth who was one step away from a jheri curl.

I sighed heavily, looking back at the computer monitor. It was in my best interest to ignore Michael's email. I pressed the delete key and watched the message vanish from my screen. Then sighed again and went back to work.

Chapter 13

"How's my favorite auntie?" Rachel said in her sugary sweet voice, which meant she wanted something.

"Seeing as how I'm your only auntie, you must mean me, and I'm fine. How's my favorite niece?"

"Well…" she hedged. "I would be doing a whole lot better if I could spend the weekend with you."

"You know you're always welcome to stay with me. But what's going on at home?"

"You know it's the first of the month and Mom is going to get her check, which means Dante is gonna be up in the crib all weekend and I just don't feel like dealin' with him anymore."

I could certainly understand how she felt. I hated visiting my sister when Dante was there. He was such a loser and my sister was a loser for allowing him to make her child feel out of place in her own home. Rachel didn't even refer to him as her dad. "Did you check with your mom to see if it's okay with her?"

"Yeah. She said she would be glad to have the peace and quiet, so she's cool with it."

"Okay. You want me to pick you up after work?"

"Yes, thanks, Auntie. I'll be ready." I could hear the big smile on my niece's face as she hung up. I decided to make it a girl's weekend and we would have a blast.

Just then, the phone rang.

"Hey, girl. Whatcha got up for tonight?" Michele asked the moment I answered the phone.

"Hey, Chele. Rachel just called and wants to spend the weekend, so I was thinking about taking her to a movie tonight and then tomorrow going to the spa. Why? Did you have something in mind?"

"Nah. I was just being nosey. Ben wants to take BJ to the movies too, but I'm sure our movie will be different than yours." Michele chuckled.

I giggled with her. "Yeah, I can imagine how excited Rach would be if I suggested some 3D animated movie. She'd have a fit."

"It definitely wouldn't be the weekend she was imagining. Anyway, since you have plans, I won't try and rope you into coming with us."

"Even if I didn't have plans, I would've passed. I really don't feel like doing much of anything these days."

"I've noticed and I'm worried about you. Why…"

I cut her off. "Hey, Chele, I still have to finish getting ready for work. I'll call you later."

"Don't try and rush me off the phone. I want to know -"

I cut her off again. "I'm not rushing you, but I do have to go. I have a meeting at 9:30 and I'm almost running late. I'll call you. Love ya. Bye." I clicked the "off" button on my cordless phone and just sat on my bed. Michele was worried about me, and I didn't intend to worry her, but I didn't feel like being social. I was much happier watching movies or cable channels.

I glanced over at the clock on my nightstand and realized I had less than 30 minutes before I needed to leave for work. I placed the phone back in its cradle and laid across my bed. I didn't have a meeting at work. Actually, my schedule was clear, so I decided to play hooky and do something just for me.

After calling in to the office and letting them know I wouldn't be in until Monday, I walked into the bathroom and decided it was finally time to tackle it and make it my personal oasis. The more I thought about my project, the more motivated I became. I went back into my bedroom and turned on the jazz station, then went over to the closet to find something to wear. I decided on a pair of capris and a tight fitting burgundy tank top, with a scoop neckline. After my shower, I put on my favorite body oil, did my makeup, styled my hair and dressed. I grabbed the keys to the Range Rover and headed for the garage.

For the first time in a long time, I was feeling pretty good, so I turned on the local R&B station and rolled down all of my windows on my short drive to Lowe's Home Improvement store. Once inside, I went straight to the bathroom displays in the center of the store. They had so many different styles to choose from that I was completely lost on where to start. As I stared at a two-person Jacuzzi jet tub, I heard a voice behind me. "I think you should buy it."

I spun around and blinked a few times. It was Rick. We'd met the summer after my first year of college and dated until the following summer. I was completely in love with him. And not only because he was gorgeous, but because he had a thuggish lifestyle at the time; and in my younger years, I found that attractive. I think back now on how foolish I was to love someone like him, but at the time it just felt right.

"Hi, Rick." This man still had the power to capture my breath. He was around 6'5" and golden brown, with almond shaped brown eyes, framed by the longest lashes I'd ever seen on a man.

"It's so good to see you, Chanelle! The years sure have been good to you," he said, as he eyed me.

I blushed. "Thank you. And they've been just as good to you," I said, checking out his muscular frame underneath his black collared polo shirt. "So, what brings you here this morning?"

"I own a home remodeling business and I'm picking up supplies for a job."

"Really? So you gave up the street life, huh?" I'd never pictured Rick doing something worthwhile with his life. I had always assumed he would either be locked up or become a victim of street crime.

"I had to. All my friends were either going to the joint or dying. Do you remember my boy, Tommy?"

I nodded.

"Well, he was sent to Jackson for murder. He received three consecutive life sentences. That was my final straw. I had to make some major changes with my life, so I took my money and started my own company."

"Very impressive. I'm glad to know that you made a career change."

"Thanks."

"Do you have a specialty?"

"My favorite room to remodel is bathrooms. Master bathrooms in particular. I don't know why, but people love their bathrooms. It's like their private sanctuary or something and I get a high off creating designs that fit their lifestyles and personalities."

"It's funny that you should say that because I decided this morning that it was time to remodel my master bath. It's so , though. How do you narrow the choices? I mean, I thought I knew what I wanted, but now I'm not so sure."

He chuckled. "That's natural. Most people stand in the middle of their space, whether it's the bathroom, bedroom, kitchen, whatever, and they dream up what they want. Then they get to the store, see all their options, and panic. A lot of times they scrap their entire project." He waited a beat before adding, "I could give you some tips if you like."

"I would love that!" I said. Then looking up at him through my lashes, I asked, "When can you come by?"

He hesitated before saying, "I was talking about giving you some pointers here, but I could stop by and take a look."

How had I jumped to the wrong conclusion? "Oh, I'm sorry. I didn't mean to be presumptuous. I guess I'm just in desperate need of help."

"It's no problem. It's what I do for a living, remember?"

He squeezed my shoulder and I felt an electrical current flow from his hand through my entire body. I couldn't believe the effect he was having on me after all these years. "Thank you. When is a good time?"

"How about this evening? I should be done with my job around 6:00. I could swing by around 6:30, if that works for you."

I thought quickly. Rachel would be there, but since it wasn't a date that wouldn't be a problem. "Six-thirty is fine." I gave him my address and home and cell phone numbers.

"It was good to see you again, Chanelle." He stared into my eyes and the moment was just a little too intense for me, so I glanced away.

I cleared my throat and then turned back to him. "Um, it was good to see you too, Rick."

"Well, I guess I'll see you tonight."

"I look forward to it."

After we said our final goodbyes, he walked away and I went back to looking at the Jacuzzi tubs. But I couldn't focus. This was the first time I'd felt a connection with anyone since Sean.

Since I was no longer in the mood to look at bathroom fixtures, I left Lowe's and headed to Michele's. It had been a while since we hung out and I missed her. I knew she would want to talk about my life and when I was going to snap out of my funk, and even though I didn't want to have that conversation, I wanted to spend time with her.

On my way to her house, I stopped by the supermarket and picked up a few steaks, a couple of chicken breasts, and pasta salad.

"Hey, Chanelle! What brings you by? And why aren't you at work?" Michele said, as she opened her front door, then stepped to the side to let me enter.

"I called in today. The place won't fall apart without me. And I missed you and wanted to spend some time with you and my godson," I said, moving toward her kitchen with the groceries.

"Well, if you want to see him, you'll have to go over to my mother's condo," Michele said, grabbing the groceries and putting them on the counter.

"What's he doing at your mom's?"

"She was missing him, so she came by earlier this morning and picked him up. What's with the raw steak?" Michele asked, removing the food from the bag.

"I had a taste for some barbecue and good conversation. And you grill up a steak like nobody else. So fire up the pit!"

"Flattery will get you everywhere. Why don't you hook up a couple of daiquiris, while I get the fire started," Michele said, as she walked to the deck in her backyard.

"You got it, girlfriend." I made the daiquiris and met Michele outside.

"So, what's been going on with you? I can't believe we haven't seen each other in a few weeks," she said.

"I know, right. Emotionally, it's been a little rough lately."

"You haven't been your usual upbeat self in quite some time, but what tipped you over the edge?" Michele asked softly.

"This whack dating life!" I chuckled lightly even though I didn't see anything funny. "I spent too much time thinking about it and it messed with my head. So, I focused on work and home, spending my time alone, not even answering your calls."

"But how could you shut me out? We've never done that to each other before."

"I know, and I apologize. I just needed some me time. But days of that turned into weeks. And before I knew it, so much time had passed...."

"I don't understand. You are a beautiful woman. You have a family and friends who love you, a great career, a beautiful home, a wonderful personality, and a body that 20-year-old women envy."

I gave her a half smile. "But none of that matters when you're lonely, especially if you want to be with someone special. Maybe you can't relate because you have Ben and BJ. You have it all. Don't get me wrong, I enjoy my life and I'm grateful for it, but I'm not getting any younger. I want the next phase of my life to start."

"What does God say in His Word about waiting? Doesn't He say something like we are to be content no matter what our circumstances? The next phase of your life will come, but you shouldn't spend this phase waiting for it and missing the fun in the phase that you're in."

"Yeah, yeah."

Michele smiled. "You know I'm right."

I rolled my eyes at my bestie and her Mary Poppins attitude. "Whatever. Guess who I saw today?"

"Who?" she asked, allowing me to switch topics.

"Rick!"

"Rick? From college?"

"The one and only. He owns a remodeling company. He's coming by tonight to check out my master bathroom and give me some tips on what I could do to change it up."

"Was he as fine as he was in college?"

"He looked better, if that's even possible."

Just then my iPhone rang and I pulled it from my purse and checked the screen. "Hey, Pumpkin," I said to Rachel. "Is everything alright?" I looked at my watch and became concerned. It was only 11:27. She must have been calling from school.

"Hi, Auntie Chanelle. Oh, yes, everything is fine. I just wanted to tell you that my friend, Maria, invited me to spend the weekend with her. I called my mom and she said it was okay. Maria's family is really cool and she has a lot of movies and games and an Xbox. Are you disappointed?"

"Of course, I'm disappointed that I won't get to spend time with my favorite niece, but we can get together later. Have fun this weekend with your friend."

"Thanks, Auntie Chanelle! You're the best."

"Yeah, yeah. Love you."

"Love you, too. Bye."

"Bye Sweetie." I set my phone down on the glass patio table. "Well, guess my plans just changed."

"Rachel's standing you up?"

"Yup. She has a friend who has lots of movies and games and an Xbox. How can I possibly compete with all of that?" I said lightheartedly.

"It's a losing battle." We laughed and then fell silent, both of us lost in our thoughts. Michele was the first to speak. "Well, since your chaperone bailed on you, can you be trusted alone with Rick?"

"Of course. Why would you even ask me that? Besides, it's not me he wants; it's my business."

Michele ignored my tone. "You don't believe that any more than I do."

"Alright, well maybe it's a combination. But for me, it's strictly about business. And Rick is someone who I know and trust."

"No, Rick is someone you used to know and trust. You haven't seen him in over a decade, so you have no idea what he's like. For all you know, he could be crazy."

"You're right," I conceded. "I'll tell you what; I'll call you as soon as he gets there and then I'll call you right after he leaves."

"Sounds like a plan. Hey, where are you going? You haven't even eaten yet..." Michele asked as I stood up.

"I know, but I don't have much of an appetite anymore. I'm going to head up to the mall. I need a couple of summer suits for work, and since I don't have to pick up Rachel from school, now is a good time to hit the shopping center. Wanna ride?"

"I wish, but since BJ is with my mom, I'm going to tell Ben to come home early. We have to take advantage of these moments when we get them! Besides, someone is leaving me with a crap load of meat that I have to finish barbecuing. I can't believe you bought all of this food and aren't going to eat any of it."

I gave her a sheepish grin. "Sorr-eee." I said, reaching down to grab my purse and phone.

"This is a total flake move and you know it."

I shrugged. "It is. But you love me anyway. Talk to you later." I blew my bestie and kiss and left.

Chapter 14

"Hello?"

"Hi, Chanelle?" a male voice asked.

"This is Chanelle. Who am I talking to?"

The voice relaxed. "Hi, this is Rick. I wanted to let you know I'm on my way."

Yes! "Okay. Well, I'll see you when you get here. Do you need directions?"

"I've actually done a couple of jobs in your subdivision. So I know exactly how to get there. I should be there in about 30 minutes."

"See ya then."

We hung up, and I inhaled deeply, and exhaled very slowly. I spent more time than I intended doing retail therapy and had only been home a few minutes. Thankfully, my house was clean, but I had planned to take a long bath to make sure my nerves were calm before arrived. I didn't want to be frazzled in any way. I dashed upstairs and hung up my new clothes, then went into the bathroom and turned on the shower. I quickly undressed and stood under the hot water, trying to unwind my mind as well as my body. This wasn't a date, but I was still anxious. I wanted him to be interested in me, even if I didn't want him back. With Michael using me for my money, Sean accepting me only as a mistress, and Lawrence seeing me as a booty-call, my self-esteem had plummeted over the last several months and I needed the attention of an attractive man to boost my ego.

After my shower, I put on my Victoria's Secret lotion and then layered the scent with their body mist. I walked into my closet and tried to figure out what to wear. I wanted to give the impression of being well put together without looking like I spent a lot of time—especially since I only had 10 minutes. Ughhh!

I needed an outfit that said, "Thanks for coming over to give me tips on remodeling my bathroom and, by the way, if you wanted to go out and grab something to eat, I'm dressed for the occasion." I finally decided on a pair of dark blue denim jeans and an orange tee. If he wanted to go out, I could throw on the matching denim jacket and my heels.

For my makeup, I went with a natural look, so I used a very light layer of foundation and mascara, a little blush on my cheeks, and a neutral lip color. I didn't have time to do much with my hair, so I pulled it back into a clip and let a few curls frame my face. I did a final check in the mirror and then started downstairs to wait for Rick.

My doorbell rang as soon as my foot touched the bottom step. I walked to the door and took a deep breath. The last time I let a man in my home, I slept with him. I really hoped and prayed that I'd behave myself this time.

"Hi, Rick!"

"Hey, Chanelle! You look fantastic." He stepped inside the door and for the second time that day he checked me out.

"Oh, stop… I can't even believe I'm letting you see me like this. I wish I'd had time to change, but I got home right before you called." Why did I lie? Did I need a compliment that badly?

"Well, you look great. Like you just stepped out of the shower."

"Ha. Right…" I gave a nervous laugh. "Um, let me take your jacket."

"Thanks," he said as he handed me his black jean jacket and I placed it on the banister. He had on the same outfit that he wore in Lowe's and he smelled a little tart. I don't know if my expression belied my thoughts, because he said, "I apologize for not changing, but my job ran a little longer than expected and I didn't want to be late."

"Mm-hmm. Not a problem, I just have to remember not to breathe too deeply." I smiled at him to let him know that it was okay that he was funky. This was definitely not going to turn into a date. I didn't even want him sitting on my couch.

He laughed. "It's nice to know you haven't changed."

"I've changed where it counts. Can I get you something to drink?"

"Pepsi would be great."

"One Pepsi coming up. Follow me."

I led him to the kitchen and pointed to the dinette set in the breakfast nook. "Have a seat, and I'll get it for you."

"So, how have things been? What have you been up to?" he asked as he sat down in one of the oak chairs.

I grabbed a couple cans of Pepsi from the refrigerator, filled two glasses from the cabinet with ice, and sat across from him. "Life's been good. No complaints." I took a sip of my Pepsi, then told him about my job and how I was steadily moving up the food chain. "How about you? Tell me about your business?"

"Well, I run it with my brother, Max. Do you remember him?"

"Oh my gosh, of course I remember Max. Is he still a playboy?"

He rolled his eyes and chuckled. "Would you expect him to be any different?"

"I guess not," I said, remembering how wild Max used to be. "How's the rest of the family?"

"Good. Everyone is good. Believe it or not, my mom still asks about you."

"Get out! Seriously?"

He nodded. "I'm serious as a heart attack. To this day, she still says you're the one who got away."

"Oh, stop." I felt my cheeks turning as red as ripe cherries. "I'm sure there's a Mrs. in the picture."

"There was, but I'm divorced." He raised his hand to show me he didn't have on a wedding band.

"I'm sorry to hear that."

"Thanks. We got married not long after I graduated from college. We went through a few tough years and then finally called it quits. We've been divorced now for a couple years. And I couldn't be happier."

"Really? Why do you say that?"

"Because I do what I want, when I want, but more than that, because I have peace in my life. When I was with my ex, we didn't click on the major issues. And we didn't communicate well. We argued about money. I liked to make it and she liked to spend it." He laughed a little.

"I can see how that would be frustrating."

"It was. When I decided to turn my life around, she wasn't supportive. She wanted the money and didn't care what I had to do to make it happen. You know what was ironic?"

"What?"

"Do you remember why you dumped me?"

"Of course. I came to my senses and realized the way we were living wasn't acceptable. But you wouldn't give up your street life."

"Right. And when I was finally ready to make that change, my wife didn't want me to."

I chuckled. "Yeah, that's nuts."

"I was so in love with her, Chanelle. I did just about anything to keep her happy. And then one day, I couldn't do it anymore. I remember the day I told her I was shifting careers and opening up my business. She wasn't down for me and gave me an ultimatum. I really wanted to choose her, but I knew that if we stayed together, she'd keep juicing me for my money and I'd never get ahead."

"Is that why you got divorced?"

"Believe it or not, it wasn't. With all that we were going through, I still wanted to be married to her. I still held out hope that we could work it out. And then she cheated on me. That was my final straw."

I fidgeted slightly in my seat and reminded myself that I was not the one who had cheated on him and he wasn't talking about me. "So, your divorce was because of an affair?"

His eyes became dark. "Yeah. If you don't have trust and honesty and a solid commitment, then why be with someone? My parents have been married forever and they've always stressed fidelity. It was drilled into me since I was a kid. Although, I think their message was lost on Max, it wasn't lost on me. But you know that from when you met them when we were in college."

I nodded, not able to speak at the moment. What would he think of me if he knew about what I'd done with Cynthia's husband? I may not have liked the woman, but she didn't deserve what I did.

He must have sensed my discomfort, though I'm sure he didn't know it was because of my life and not his. He let out a nervous laugh. "I apologize for telling you all that. I know I said way more than what you wanted to hear."

"That's okay. Sometimes it's good to get it out," I said, returning my focus to him.

"Maybe, but I'm still embarrassed."

"Don't be." I reached across the table and gently placed my hands over his. First he looked down and I wondered if I was being too forward, but then he looked into my eyes.

"Thank you, Chanelle."

Quietly, I said, "Rick, no matter how much time passes we will always have a friendship. Besides, back in the day, we used to talk about everything."

"We did, didn't we?"

"Yeah," I nodded. "The only problem we had in our relationship was the way you made money. If you'd have given up the drug dealing, we probably would have stayed together." *And I'd have my white picket fence, my kids, and my dog,* I thought to myself, but wouldn't dare say out loud.

He continued to use my eyes as the window to my heart. "I appreciate you listening. Like I said, my mother always knew you were a very special woman. I agreed with her back in college and I agree with her now." His words made me blush and I pulled my hands away and turned from him. I was trying to understand this crazy chemistry we still seemed to have.

"Thanks." I didn't know what else to say. "Are you ready to take a look at my bathroom?"

He read my cue and our conversation took on a business tone. "Sure. Lead the way."

We stood from the table and he followed me up the stairs. Once inside, he began his inspection and began asking me questions. "So, do you have any ideas on what you want?"

I shook my head. "The only thing I know for sure is that I want a two-person Jacuzzi tub."

"Two-person, huh? So, is that because you're planning for your future or because there's someone in your life?"

"That's a presumptuous question."

"Hey, I spilled my guts in five minutes flat. I'm just hoping you'll share something too, so I don't feel like such a fool."

"As your friend, Rick, you don't need to feel like a fool around me." Then I added, "But as your potential client, my reason for wanting a two-person Jacuzzi is my business. Okay?"

I think Rick was a little stunned by my response and, actually, I was too. It would have taken a butcher knife to cut the thick tension in the air.

Rick cleared his throat and in his most professional voice, he shared some options with me. I tried to listen intently, since it seemed that he had some very good suggestions. But I couldn't fully concentrate on what he was saying, because I was too busy replaying our conversation. He'd shared so much about his relationship and I had shut him down.

And I didn't know why. All I knew was that I was officially confused. I had been anxious and excited about him coming over and now I needed him to leave. I wondered if I could even hire him because things were just weird with us.

"Chanelle? Chanelle?"

"Huh?"

"Are you okay? I've been talking to you, but I'm not sure you were listening. I was asking what you thought about shades of green."

"Green? Hmmm. Can I think about it? Actually, can I be honest with you?" I faced him and, although he looked puzzled, he nodded. "I feel a little awkward. First you tell me about your broken marriage and I felt you needed to let it out, so that was okay. Then you ask me a playful question about my two-person Jacuzzi and I have a reaction that I can't explain. Rick, you've been in my house less than 30 minutes and my head is spinning." I laughed slightly.

Rick paused a moment. "I agree that our conversation was different. How about we start over? No more personal questions or discussions. Let's keep it strictly about business. I firmly believe that I can do an excellent job with your bathroom and I want your business. I believe that I still know what you like." When I raised my eyebrow, he quickly added, "You know what I mean. You had excellent taste in college and judging by the way your home looks, you still do."

"Thank you. This bathroom is the only part of my house that I haven't redone. How about you draw a sketch of your plans and bring them by next Saturday? If I like it, and your quote is reasonable, then the job is yours. Deal?" I extended my hand.

"Deal." Instead of shaking my hand, he grabbed it, pulled me toward him, and gave me a hug that short-circuited my senses.

I didn't know what to do, so I hugged him back and felt the same electrical current that I'd felt earlier. We stood for a moment locked in a warm embrace until I reluctantly pulled away and looked him in his eyes. "I think you'd better go."

His voice was deep and raspy as he forced himself to release me. "I understand." He cleared his throat. "I'll call you once the drawings are complete. Do you mind if I take a few pictures of your bathroom?"

"Sure. Take all the time you need. I'll be downstairs." As he slipped a small camera from his pocket, I headed down the steps to safety. Rick came down about 10 minutes later, picked up his jacket, and headed straight for the front door.

I followed him and he turned to face me before opening the door. "It was great to see you again, Chanelle. I hope you know that I'm not the same man you dated years ago. I've grown and matured. I'd love to take you to dinner sometime, but I'll understand if you have a man or you're just not interested." I felt his eyes pierce straight through me. I knew he wanted some kind of reassurance from me, but I couldn't give it to him.

"Let's stay focused on the job. Okay?" My eyes pleaded with him to drop the subject of us and stick to business.

"Okay. I'll call you sometime this week." And with that he let himself out.

Chapter 15

I sat at my desk in my office and gazed out the window lost in thought, which was something I often did when I was working through a problem. Only this time, my issue had nothing to do with work. It was all about Rick. It had been three days since he came over and I was just as confused now as I was the day he was there. He'd been on my mind a lot. I realized that I'd made the whole night into a huge deal. I had decided that when he called, I was going to act like all was normal and move forward. Hopefully, he would follow suit. I had also decided that if he asked me out again that I would say yes. Michele had told me that I'd made an issue out of nothing. And she was right. Rick had always treated me well.

My assistant lightly tapped on my door. "Chanelle? You have a delivery." She had a huge smile on her face and I wondered what it could be.

I quickly stood up and followed her out of the office. The bright floral arrangement that sat atop her desk left me without words. There were 2 dozen yellow and white roses. Who in the world would have sent me flowers?

I searched the bouquet for the card, anxious to find out who I needed to thank. Patty stared at me, waiting for me to read the card aloud, but I chose to read it by myself, so I said, "These are gorgeous! I'm taking them into my office."

"Gorgeous is an understatement, Boss Lady! Some dude must really be feelin' you. I wish my old man would send me flowers one day. You know, he didn't even send flowers after my hip surgery? Come to think of it—"

I cut her off. "Patty, would you mind terribly if we discussed this another time? These are kinda heavy and I want to set them down on my desk."

"No problem. You go on and enjoy the flowers. And give that man an extra special Thank Ya'," she said, giving me a wink.

I hurried inside my office, and kicked the door closed with my foot. I briskly stepped to my desk and placed the bouquet on the corner, pulled the card, and took a seat on my couch.

The card simply read "What if…"

That was it.

I flipped it over. Nothing. Puzzled, I got up and searched the bouquet for some sign of who could have sent it. Nothing. I sighed deeply and sat back on my couch. There was no one in my life who should be sending me flowers. I leaned over and picked up the phone on the table next to the couch and called Michele.

Hey, girl," I said, the moment she answered. "What you got up for today?"

"Just working on the books for our business while BJ is at preschool."

I envied her for being able to work from home. "Wanna meet for lunch?"

"Sounds like a plan. How about we go to Champs since it's halfway between me and you?"

"Cool." We agreed to meet at the bar and grill at noon, giving me almost no time to do any work. Which was good because I couldn't concentrate anyway. I kept staring at my flowers and the cryptic card.

"What if? What if?" I said softly to myself. What if what? What if we were together? What if I love you? What if I'm crazy? What on earth did "What if?" mean?

Just then Patty buzzed me on my office line. "Uh, Boss Lady... you have a call on Line 1."

"Who is it?"

"He won't leave a name. But he says you'll know what it's about and you'll want to take his call."

"O-K..., put him through."

"Yes, Boss Lady."

"Hello?"

"Is this Chanelle Slate?" a gruff voice asked.

"You placed the call. Shouldn't you know?"

The caller let out a creepy laugh. "You want to play it like that? Okay. My client has hired me because my client wants revenge against you."

"Yeah, right. Is this a joke?"

"I'm far from a joke."

I rolled my eyes. "Sure you are. Did Michael set this up? If so, you tell him it's not funny."

"Look, I don't know who Michael is. My client prefers to remain anonymous at this time. But understand this, Ms. Slate: at the right time, all will be revealed."

"Mm-hmm. Well, Mr. Scary man, I'm very busy. So either you tell me who's behind this unfunny joke or I'm hanging up."

"I don't think you understand, this is not a -"

Click. I hung up. I didn't know who thought it would be amusing to prank me at work, but it was highly unprofessional and I was agitated.

I buzzed Patty and told her to hold all my calls, then I snapped a picture of my flowers, put the card in my purse, and headed out to meet Michele.

⚮

"Girl, you are not going to believe my morning," I said, taking a seat at the table and reaching for the drink menu.

She raised an eyebrow. "Um, aren't you still on the clock?"

"What? You mean this?" I asked, pointing to the drink menu. "When I tell you about my day, you'll understand why I need this." We chuckled, then placed our orders with the waitress who'd arrived with our silverware and water.

"So what's going on?"

"Look at this." I pulled out my cell phone and showed her the picture of my flowers.

"Those are gorgeous! Who sent them?"

"Beats me. This is all that came with them." I handed her the card.

"What if?" She flipped it over.

"I did the same thing. That's all there is. Two words."

"Do you think they're from Rick?"

I shook my head. "Why would Rick be sending me flowers? Especially after our evening ended so weird. Nah, I don't think it's him."

"Could it be Sean?"

"I thought about it and if it was right after he moved, then maybe. But too much time has passed for it to be him. And besides, the last time we spoke, I told him not to call me anymore. And he didn't. Which honestly, I thought he'd try at least one more time," I said, shrugging. "So it's certainly not him."

She nodded. "You have a point. What about Michael?"

"Chile, please," I laughed. "Maybe black roses, but not yellow and white."

Michele chuckled with me. "Rocco would have a fit if he found out that Michael sent you flowers."

I continued laughing and said, "Exactly. Especially if he knew that Michael was thinking he may not be gay after all." Then my laughter subsided. "So I have no idea where they came from. I'm not dating anybody. And then get this," I said, changing subjects, "I got a prank phone call."

"Seriously? At our age? Who's playing games on the phone?"

"No clue. They said some craziness about being hired by their client to get revenge on me."

"That's nonsense," she said, taking a bite of the jalepeno popper that had just been placed on our table.

"I know. I tried to find out who was behind it, and then I got so irritated that I just hung up."

"Do you think the call is related to the flowers?"

"Hmm, not really. I mean, the flowers were beautiful. The call was mean. The two don't go together. Maybe the flowers were delivered to me by accident."

"I'm sure they were for you. You just haven't figured out who sent them yet."

"Hey, Chanelle, it's great to see you, baby!" an unfortunately recognizable male voice said, disturbing our conversation.

I felt like a rock had settled in my stomach as I turned toward the voice. "Hi, Lawrence."

"You ready to go out on another date with Big Daddy?"

I had to choke back the vomit that was suddenly in my mouth. "Lawrence, you have a woman. And besides that, we have nothing in common." I held up my thumb and forefinger in the shape of a circle to emphasize my point.

"Oh, so it's like that?"

I frowned. "Of course it's like that. If you see me again, just pretend you didn't."

"Okay, okay," he said, holding his hands up and backing away from the table. "Hey, Michele, how you doin'? You alright?"

"Yes, I'm fine."

"Alright, cool, cool. I'll holla," he said, and turned and walked back to his bar stool.

Michele and I looked at each other, shaking our heads. That was bizarre," she said.

"Bizarre has been my life lately."

We giggled as the waitress brought our meals and my drink.

"Now do you see why I need this?"

"Girl, with your life, you should have made it a double."

Chapter 16

I stared at my computer screen, but wasn't really seeing the words. Since that first call on Monday, I'd received a call every day after. I was thankful that it was Thursday and the weekend would soon be here, because I was beginning to stress a little. Initially I thought it was a joke, but the tone of the calls had escalated and I was becoming concerned that this was serious.

"Boss Lady, you have a call on Line 1," Patty said through our intercom.

"Is it the same guy?"

"Sounds like it. Do you want me to take a message?"

"Yes. And bring me the Simmons file, please."

"You got it, Boss Lady."

I turned my attention back to the document I was working on anda moment later, my cell on my desk rang. I glanced at the number and it said "Unknown".

I was cautious as I answered. "Hell-o."

"So you're avoiding my calls now?" that nasty voice said.

"What do you want with me?"

"I told you before. My client has paid me to get revenge on you."

I started shaking internally. "And I've asked you before, who is your 'client' and what does your client think I did?"

"You should already know."

"What do you have to gain by hurting me?"

"Money. And since I don't know you, I won't cry over you."

"Well, is there anything I can do to make it right with your client?"

"It's too late for that. For now, my warning to you is to watch your back. I know where you live, where you work, what you drive, and who's important to you. And if you think about calling the cops, your precious little Rachel will pay the price. I'll be back in touch. Make sure you take my call." And with that, the caller hung up. I still held the phone while I racked my brain trying to think who would want to hurt me. I was a good person with a ton of friends and no known enemies -- till now.

I swallowed the lump in my throat, while tears pooled in the corners of my eyes.

As I sat trying to figure out what my next steps needed to be, Patty entered my office. Looking down at the papers in her hand, she said, "Boss Lady, here's the file you requested. Do you need anything else?"

I spoke softly. "That'll be all. Thank you."

She finally looked at me. "Oh, my God, Boss Lady, you look white as a ghost! Are you okay?"

I blinked rapidly as I tried to focus on Patty. "Uh…yeah… yeah… I'm fine."

"Does this have anything to do with the man who keeps calling you?"

I nodded. "Yes, he said he wants to kill me," I whispered.

"Why would someone want to kill you?" Patty practically screamed.

I jumped up from my chair and quickly crossed the floor so I could close my office door. "Shh… keep your voice down. I don't want the whole office to know."

"I'm so sorry, Ms. Boss Lady. I just hate that someone wants to hurt you. You are one of the sweetest people I know. Do you think it's real or is somebody pullin' your leg?"

I slumped against my office door. "I have no idea what's going on, Patty. I didn't think it was real at first, but he's been calling me all week and now I just don't know." I started to feel my legs betray me as I slid down the door.

Patty swift ran to my side, put her arm around my waist and led me to my couch. After she helped me sit, she said, "Stay right here. I'm gonna get you some water." She left my office and was back in what felt like seconds.

"Here, drink this." She handed me the cup, but my hands were trembling so badly that I spilled half of the water in my lap. Patty took the cup from me and held it to my lips so I could take a few sips of what remained.

"Thank you."

"You don't need to thank me. I'd do anything for you, Boss Lady," Patty said, as she sat next to me and opened her arms. I put my head on her shoulder and cried. And cried.

"Chanelle! Are you okay? What happened?" I must've been delirious, because I could swear I was hearing Michele's voice. But when I looked up, she was standing in front of me. I had no idea how long I had cried on Patty's shoulder.

"How—how did you know something was up?"

"Patty called me. She said you got a threatening phone call and you wouldn't stop crying on her."

I pushed away from Patty, narrowing my eyes into thin slits and clinching my jaw. "When did you call Michele?"

"I'm so sorry, Boss Lady, but I know that Michele is your best friend and she would want to know and she would know what to do. I called her when I went to get your water."

Michele interjected, "Don't you get mad at Patty. She only called me because she cares about you. And you would have called yourself if you weren't crying. Now, what is going on?"

Michele attempted to sit next to me, but I was suddenly antsy and jumped up, pacing my office floor. "I have no idea. Every day this week, I've been called by this, this *man* who keeps threatening me." I wrapped my arms around myself and tried to stop the cold that was overpowering me.

"Are you talking about that prank phone call you got on Monday?"

I nodded.

"Why didn't you tell me he called again?"

"I don't know. I – I just thought if I ignored him, he'd go away. But today, when Patty asked if I wanted take his call, I said no, and asked her to take a message. And then, he called me on my cell phone! He has my cell number! This, this isn't a sick joke. It's a sick reality."

Michele let out an audible gasp. "Oh my God!"

My tears resumed their paths down my cheeks. "I know," I said, my voice was barely a whisper. "He said he knows where I live, what I drive, who my family is." I stopped pacing and faced my best friend. "Michele, he called Rachel by her name…"

"I'm calling the police," Michele said as she rose from the couch and headed toward my desk phone.

"No," I screamed and raced in front of her, snatching the phone out of her hand as she picked it up.

"Are you crazy?" Michele looked at me as though I'd grown another head.

"No, I'm not crazy. But he knows my family. And they're in danger if I say anything. Let me handle this on my own. Please," I pleaded with her.

"Well you can't be a sitting duck, waiting for him to hurt you. That's nonsense. And you're too smart for that."

"I'd rather he hurt me than do something to my family. No police. Period. I'll handle this on my own."

Michele was silent for what felt like hours. "Not on your own." When I opened my mouth to object, she raised her hand. "Let me finish. Not on your own. But no police. For now. I will not promise you that I won't call them at some point. And I am telling Ben."

"Just make sure he doesn't call the cops. I'm serious, Michele. This is my life."

"What I'll promise is this: if Ben and I decide to call the cops, we will tell you first. What you have to promise is to tell me everything."

I nodded to indicate that I agreed with her terms.

"Do you have any idea what this could be about?"

I shook my head. "I honestly don't. I'm completely lost on this one. I mean, maybe Rocco, but I can't imagine he'd go this far."

"Do you think it's business related?" Patty interjected, reminding us that she was still in the room. "Ever since you won that huge account earlier this year, you've had a lot of your competition mad as heck."

I paused. "I hadn't thought about that."

"Even the Simmons account was a major score and upset a lot of people when they switched firms and signed under you," she continued.

I glanced at the file she'd placed on my desk. Patty was right about my growing portfolio. The account that I landed earlier in the year with Sean's help had opened a lot of huge doors for me and aggravated many of my rivals in the industry.

I ran my hand through my curls. "I don't know, Patty. Yes, a lot of people are angry, but we're all professionals and everything was just business."

"Well, I didn't say anything before because I know you don't get into office gossip But I was talkin' to Sandra in the break room the other day. She was tellin' me that Heather told her that Marisa was pissed off when Mr. Jeffries promoted you to partner and started giving you the larger accounts."

"Are you kidding me! I didn't do anything dirty or underhanded to win these accounts," I said, pointing at the file. "Nor did I do anything shady to make partner! And besides, Marisa's in line to be promoted, but she has to pay her dues like everybody else."

"Calm down, Boss Lady. You're probably right. Maybe that was a stretch. Or maybe someone doesn't know that you've been winning your accounts fair and square." She stood and said, "Anyway, I'll give you two some privacy. But please let me know if there's anything I can do."

I was touched by Patty's genuine concern. "Thank you. But this is my battle to fight."

"Well, just let me know. Me and my ol' man got yo back fo sho."

I smiled and then giggled a little. "I know you do. And I appreciate you both."

It was times like this when I was glad I made the decision, against conventional wisdom, to keep Patty onboard.

She returned the smile and left my office, silently closing the door behind her. But just as Michele and I sat down on my couch, Patty burst back in, clearly in a panic. "Boss Lady, Michele, you gotta see this!" she exclaimed.

Michele and I turned to each, and I knew the fear in her eyes mirrored the fear in mine. We jumped up together and quickly followed Patty out of my office. We were stopped cold in our tracks by the sight in front of us. At the entrance to my office suite was a dead rat with a note pinned to its lifeless chest and held in place by a sharp pocket knife. Just the sight before my eyes tied my stomach into several small knots.

"Oh, my God! I think I'm gonna be sick." I almost passed out, but Patty was thinking on her toes.

"Boss Lady, if anybody sees this, it could kill your career!" Patty said frantically. She grabbed a sheet of copy paper and her trash can. Holding her breath, she picked up the rodent and threw it in the garbage, but not before unpinning the letter. "Do you want me to read it?"

I was in a trance. "I don't understand. Who is doing this to me? This is a nightmare."

"Yes, it's a nightmare and it's absolutely ridiculous that you won't let us call the police," Michele said, snapping me out of my comatose state. "Chanelle, this is serious. Someone is sending you a very strong message. Are you sure you have no idea who's behind this?"

"I don't lie to you. I may not tell you everything, but I don't lie. As God is my witness, I have no idea what is going on. But I do know that Patty is right. I can't let anyone see this." Fortunately, my office was at the end of the hall and was relatively secluded.

There was no huge risk of anyone just passing by. But I was still worried that someone saw the delivery. I had no idea how I would explain what was going on if someone asked. I just hoped and prayed no one would bring it up.

I turned and went back into my office, with Patty and Michele right behind me.

"Patty," Michele began, "let me see the note, please." Patty handed it to her and she read it silently.

"Well, what does it say?" I asked impatiently.

She hesitated, as she glanced at me with a look of trepidation in her eyes. "Well...." she hedged.

"What does it say?" I snapped.

She looked back down at the note and took a deep breath. "I despise you, Chanelle. You will pay. And you'll pay with your life."

I gulped and slumped in my chair, while tears slid back down my cheeks.

Chapter 17

After Michele read the note, I realized I physically couldn't take anymore. What in the heck was going on? I wanted to be alone, but I knew Patty and Michele wouldn't leave my side, so I said, "Patty, I think you should go back to your desk so we can look as normal and possible. And Michele, would you mind getting me a bottle of water?"

"No problem," they said in unison.

"Michele, the vending machine is at the end of the hall," Patty offered, giving her directions.

As soon as they left my office and Michele had gone down the hall, I grabbed my purse and keys and ran toward the bank of elevators. I felt claustrophobic and I had to escape. I heard Patty calling my name, but turning around wasn't an option.

When I reached the elevators, I pushed the "down" button multiple times, even though it had already been pushed by the person who was standing there staring at me like he was looking at a lunatic. As soon as the doors opened, I stepped in and pressed the button for the parking garage. When I reached my BMW, my cell phone rang and I knew it was Michele.

I pushed her to voicemail and sent her a quick text, letting her know I was going home and that I just needed some time to myself. I'd call her later. We texted back and forth a few times until I was comfortable that she wouldn't follow me.

It was no surprise that I arrived home faster than a NASCAR driver. I parked in my garage and scurried into my house. Once inside, I set my alarm and ran upstairs. I needed the sanctuary of my bedroom. I left a trail of clothes from the bottom of the stairs to my bed. I put on my most comfortable flannel pajamas, even though it was the middle of summer. As I was contemplating never leaving my house again, I drifted off to sleep and was awakened by the shrill of my home phone ringing.

"Michele, I don't feel like talking." I said groggily, as I answered the phone.

"Excuse me? Chanelle?" a deep voice responded.

"Oh, I'm sorry. I thought you were… never mind. Who's calling?" I had a splitting headache and just wanted to get rid of whoever was on the line.

"This is Rick. Chanelle?" Rick sounded truly puzzled.

I tried to think of something clever to say, but my mind was fried. The most I could come up with was a halfhearted apology. "I'm sorry. I thought you were someone else, and I didn't check the caller ID before I answered."

"Oh, no problem. Is everything okay?"

"Uh, yeah. Yeah. I just…" I toyed with the idea of telling him what had happened today, but decided against it. "I just had a very long day, that's all. So what's up?" I hoped he wouldn't push it and let me change the subject.

"Well, I have the designs for your bathroom. I've created three different options and I wanted to set up some time to show you."

"That's great, Rick. Um, I thought we were set for Saturday?"

"We are, but I was kind of hoping to show you sooner. I think you'll be very pleased with the designs. I thought maybe I could come by tonight unless you have plans."

I was certainly in no mood to entertain. But now that the adrenaline of the day had worn off, I was afraid to be alone. Maybe having Rick come by would be a good thing. "I guess tonight is okay. What time?" I asked wearily.

"I'm literally around the corner. Have you eaten? I could grab some Thai food and be there in 20 minutes," he said.

Despite my awful day, I had to admit to myself that I was a little excited to see him. And maybe focusing on my bathroom redesign was just what I needed. I felt my mood lifting slightly. "I haven't eaten and I absolutely love Thai food. There's a really good restaurant down the street from me. It's called Thai Chi. Have you heard of it?"

"Have I heard of it? It's my favorite! I'll see you soon."

"Sounds good." We disconnected the call. I desperately wanted to keep on my flannel pajamas, but I knew better. I dragged myself from my bed and went to my chest of drawers. I threw on some old workout clothes and mismatched footies and laid back across my bed. I dozed off again and was startled by the sound of my doorbell. Before I headed downstairs, I searched for my cell phone and remembered that I had left it on the kitchen counter. I made a mental note to grab it.

"That was delicious!" I said, licking the last of the sweet and sour sauce off my fingers.

Rick smiled. "I'm glad you enjoyed it."

"It was just what I needed," I said as we sat on the sofa in front of my glass cocktail table in the den. I glanced over at Rick and noticed he was studying me. "What? Why are you staring at me?" I asked, using my fingernail as a toothpick, thinking maybe I had a piece of chicken satay stuck between my teeth.

"Nothing."

"Don't say 'nothing'. You were staring at me for a reason." It was at that moment that I glanced at my reflection in the cocktail table and noticed that my hair was matted and my eyes were red and puffy. "Never mind. I think I just figured out why you were staring. Why didn't you tell me I was hit?"

"Because I don't see a 'hit' woman, as you describe yourself. I see a beautiful woman who had a rough day."

His compliment warmed my heart. "Thank you. I did have a rough day."

"Do you want to talk about it?" he asked gently.

I took a deep breath and contemplated for the second time that day about what to tell him. Rick must have sensed my hesitation and tried to put me at ease. "I only ask because I'm concerned about you. You're obviously in distress."

"Maybe some other time we'll discuss it. Right now, you being here and keeping me company is helping me more than you realize." I lowered my chin because I didn't want him to see me well up.

But he leaned toward me, gently cupped my face and forced me to look him in the eyes. "I'm here for you."

"I know you are, Rick. And I thank you." I squeezed his hand and composed myself. "Now, let's look at those drawings."

Rick stood. "I left them in the truck. I'll be right back." As he walked to the front door, I grabbed our plates and dropped them off in the kitchen. When I saw my phone on the counter, I noticed that I'd missed seven calls.

That was a bit much, even for Michele and I wondered why she didn't call me at home, but I dialed my voicemail ready to hear her chastise me for taking off and not calling the police.

The first five messages were no surprise. Just Michele, Ben, and Patty. It was the sixth message that sent chills from my head to my mismatched socks. "I saw you pull into your driveway. How'd you like your special delivery?"

Oh, my God. This whack job was telling the truth when he said he knew where I lived. And he was outside my house! I pressed 9 to save the message and then I listened to message #7. "So, is that your new boyfriend? He can't save you from your fate."

Rick strolled into the kitchen and stopped short when he saw me. He sprinted to my side and asked, "What happened? You look like something spooked you!"

I finally opened up to him. "Someone is stalking me. I don't know who it is or why he's doing it. But he knows where I live and he's watching me. For all I know, he's outside now, because he left me a message and said he saw you."

Rick raced back to the front door with me right behind him. Standing on my porch, we caught a glimpse of a dark-colored four-door sedan speeding off.

"That must have been him," I said, as we came back into the house and I led him to the den.

"Why would someone be stalking you?"

"I already told you I don't know," I snapped.

"When did it start?"

"Monday." I held back my tears and recapped the events of my week.

Without words, Rick wrapped his arms around me. I was consoled by his strength and concern and the dam inside me broke. I cried harder than I had ever cried in my life and, when I finished, he wiped away my tears.

As I looked at his tear soaked chest, I felt like a little girl when I sniffed and said, "I'm sorry I got your shirt wet."

He smiled at me with tenderness in his eyes. "It's just a shirt." Then his countenance changed. "I know you said you weren't calling the police, but I really think you need to reconsider. This man is dangerous. You can't handle this by yourself."

I pushed away from him and shook my head. "I can't call them! He said he'll hurt Rachel. Whatever I did, or someone thinks I did, or I'm doing, I can't let my family pay for it. No, I just have to figure this out on my own."

He pulled me back to him. "I'm spending the night. And before you bother arguing with me, it's not up for discussion. I'll sleep on the couch in the den. Where do you keep the sheets?"

I remembered how protective he was when we were in college and there was no way I'd win if I protested. It was reassuring to know that at least some things about him had remained the same. So I said, "I'll get them."

I picked up the trail of clothes I'd left when I got home and went upstairs to grab linen for my sofa bed. Rick went back out to his truck and came back in as I was making up the sofa bed. When I finished, I thanked him for staying and kissed him on the cheek. As I headed back up the stairs, I heard a thud on the table. I turned around to see a 9 millimeter handgun. Yup, some things remained the same.

Chapter 18

"Wake up, Sunshine."

"Go away," I mumbled, even though I was flattered that he remembered my nickname. I was face down under layers of blankets and I wasn't ready to re-enter the world.

"Come on. It's 2:30."

"Why are you waking me up at 2:30 in the morning?"

"It's not 2:30 a.m. It's 2:30 p.m."

My eyes opened as wide as I could get them since I was still groggy. "You're kidding."

Rick sat on the side of my bed and placed his hand on top of back. "I'm not kidding. I've been checking on you every hour on the hour. Did you know you snore like a sailor? And you drool a little, too." He laughed.

I peeked my head out from under my blankets and gave him a playful push. "I do not snore...and I definitely do not drool."

"That's what you think. But your wet pillow says differently."

I cut my eyes at him. "Whatever!"

He stood. "Come on. You have to get up and eat something."

I sat up in bed. "I'm not hungry. Did you see the car again last night?" I asked, afraid to hear the answer.

The smile left Rick's face and his eyes became dark. "Yeah, I did. He was here around 5:30 this morning. I was at least able to get a better look at the car. It's a late model Buick. Either navy blue or black. And it has a big dent by the left fender."

"Were you able to get the license plate?"

"Unfortunately, I couldn't see it. I don't think he was expecting to see my truck in your driveway because he sped past."

Tears welled up in the corners of my eyes and slid down my cheeks. "I'm glad you were here, Rick. I don't know what would have happened if I was alone."

Rick knelt in front of my bed and gently wiped away my tears. "I'm not going to let anything happen to you. Until we get to the bottom of this, you're going to have a live-in houseguest. And before you object, it's not up for discussion."

I vehemently shook my head. "Uh uh. I can't ask you to do that."

"You didn't ask me. I'm going to be honest with you." He paused for a moment as if he were contemplating his next words. "When I saw you in the store, I found myself attracted to you all over again. And I do want to get to know you again. But that's not what this is about. I don't want to see anything bad happen to you."

I looked at him and knew he was being genuine. I let out a big sigh. I appreciated that he was taking charge, so I gave in. "Okay," I said simply.

"What? That's it? No fight?"

I gave him the brightest smile I could muster. "That's it. I don't have any fight left in me. I'm scared. So, if you're offering to protect me, then I'm going to accept."

He kissed my forehead and sent shockwaves pulsating through my body. "Thank you for trusting me. Now, I have something planned for us today. So, get up and get dressed," he said, as he stood again and headed toward my bedroom door.

I thought about work. "Oh, no! I didn't call in."

"Settle down. Patty called to check on you. I only answered your phone because I didn't want to wake you and figured your friends were worried. Anyway, she told your boss that you had an emergency and wouldn't be in today and next week. She also said she got rid of the rat, but took a picture of it and kept the note in case you needed it. Michele called you, too. I told her you were sleeping and you'd call her when you woke up. I'll see you downstairs." And with that, he left my room.

I called Patty to thank her and let her know I was okay and then I placed a quick call to Mr. Jeffries. It was my responsibility to make sure my job was protected.

"Hi, Alana," I said to his executive assistant when she answered. "This is Chanelle. Is Mr. Jeffries around?"

"Hi, Chanelle! Yes, hold on a moment." I waited while she transferred my call.

"Chanelle, how are you? Patty said you had a family emergency. I hope everyone is okay."

"Yes, we're fine. I, um, just have a couple things I need to handle. I'll be back as soon as I can."

"No worries. I know if something is keeping you away from the office, then it must be serious. I'm here for you if you need me."

I had the best boss in the world. "Thank you, Sir."

After a couple minutes of small talk, I hung up and called Michele.

"Hey, how are you doing today?" she asked.

"Eh, I've had better days. Last night the stalker was outside my house."

"Oh no! Did you see him?"

"I didn't. Thankfully, Rick was here."

"I figured that out when he answered your phone."

"He came by last night and I told him what's been going on and he offered to stay with me for a few days."

I could hear her raising her eyebrows. "Oh really?"

"Yes, really. There's nothing going on. And this is a blessing, so don't worry. I'm a lot safer with Rick here than being by myself."

"O-K. You know I've got your back and I support you. But I do still disagree with you about the police."

"Now you sound like Rick. And it's not that I won't ever do it. I just have to think this through. I can't put any of my family in danger. I'd never forgive myself."

"What about Steve?"

"Your brother Steve?"

"Yeah. What if we call Steve? He's a cop. He might have some suggestions for you."

"Hmm. Let me think about it."

"Okay. I won't push it right now. Especially since I know you're not alone."

"Thanks. Rick says he has something planned for us today."

"Oooh, a date."

"I doubt that. Knowing Rick, it could be anything." We chuckled and lightened the mood.

After agreeing to periodically check in with her throughout the day, I hung up and dragged myself out of bed.

I desperately wanted to stay in my room, but I was curious to know what Rick had planned. I showered, dressed, and headed downstairs. As I sat at the kitchen table, Rick brought me a grilled ham and cheese sandwich, a cup of tomato soup, and a glass of apple juice. "Aren't you going to eat?" I asked, as he sat across from me with a cup of coffee.

"I ate a little something earlier."

"Oh. Well, thank you." I blessed my food and took a big bite of my sandwich. "Mmm... This takes me back to my days as a child. I ate it almost every Saturday at my grandparent's home."

"I remember. You used to eat it when we were in college."

I paused with my sandwich in midair. "I had completely forgotten about that. I can't believe you remembered."

"I remember a lot of things about you, Chanelle. You've been in and out of my thoughts since college. I'm glad we're having a chance to reconnect."

I was too, but I wasn't sure what to say, so I switched topics. "What do you have planned for us today?"

"It's a surprise."

"Oooh... I like surprises."

"I remembered that, too. While you finish eating, I'm going to make a couple calls for work and then do a quick walk around the house."

I was grateful to Rick for everything that he was doing for me and I was anxious to get to my surprise, so I wolfed down my meal and was ready to go in record time. After reassuring me that no one was around my house, I grabbed my purse, and keys, then we headed outside to his truck.

I was happy that for at least a little while, I could concentrate on something other than the madness that what was happening to me.

"Are you serious? This is my surprise?" I asked as I stared straight ahead.

"Yes. This is something you need to learn how to do."

I could feel Rick's eyes on me, but I refused to face him. "There's no way I'm going inside," I said, folding my arms.

"There's no way you're not going inside," he said, unfolding my arms. "Now come on." He unlocked the doors and got out.

I stayed seated. I was not going inside that building. Rick walked around to my side of the truck and opened my door. "Come on. This is going to be good for you."

"I'm scared. I've never done this before."

"There's a first time for everything. And I'm going to help you. But this is something that you really need to do."

I inhaled deeply, then let out a long, slow breath.

While I contemplated my next move, Rick extended his hand. "Do you want my arm to fall off?"

I tried my best not to crack a smile. "Do not quote Billie D. Williams in *Lady Sings the Blues* to me. This is no time for jokes." I refolded my arms.

Rick reached inside, unfolded my arms again, and tried to coax me out of the truck. After about five minutes of bantering back and forth, I had no choice but to give in. I was stubborn, but he had me beat. "Okay. I'll go in on one condition."

"What's that?"

"We go at my pace. No matter how slow that may be."

"Deal."

I finally got out and together we walked inside the "Firing Line," a first-rate gun range. I had secretly always wanted to learn how to shoot, but I was terrified of guns. And I was even more afraid of the implication. Rick must have believed that I was truly in danger. Otherwise, why else would he force me to learn how to shoot a gun?

As soon as we walked through the door, I saw cases upon cases of guns. Different styles and calibers. The sight was overwhelming and I subconsciously grabbed Rick's hand. He briefly looked down at our entwined fingers and smiled. In the background, we could hear people shooting in the practice area and every time I heard a gun fire, I flinched. This was definitely not the kind of surprise I had in mind.

Rick told one of the associates that this was my first time and that we needed to rent a practice gun. He suggested that I start with a .22 caliber, so I could get used to the feel and power. I followed his lead, since I had no idea what he was talking about. He also rented ear and eye protectors for us and then took me to the range. Each practice space was separated by metal partitions. After Rick gave me a lesson on the proper way to load, reload, and hold the firearm, it was time to shoot.

"Okay, Chanelle. Pay attention. Do you see how I'm standing?" I nodded and he continued. "You stand with your legs a little apart so you can keep your balance. Now notice how I hold my hands." I watched him intently and wondered how in the world did he expect me to imitate what he was doing. The sound of him firing that first round startled me. But with each shot, I relaxed a little. That is, until he turned and asked, "Are you ready?"

"Not really, but I'll try," I said with great reservation. He handed the gun to me and my entire body tensed.

"You'll do fine." He stood behind me and put his arms around me. He placed his hands on top of mine, as he positioned me to fire my first round.

I was trying to focus on what he was saying, but I was jittery; partly because I was about to shoot my first gun, but mostly because we were so close. I could smell his cologne and feel his breath on my neck. Focus Chanelle. Focus.

"Go ahead. Pull the trigger."

"Okay." I closed my eyes and squeezed. The kickback from the gun made me jump slightly.

"Not bad. How did it feel?"

"It was okay. Different than I expected."

"Now, do it again," he commanded.

"Okay." I closed my eyes and squeezed again. With each shot, I became more comfortable.

After a few rounds, he came from behind me. "This time, you do it on your own and I'll watch."

I took a deep breath and nodded, then repeated my same process.

"Good job. But were your eyes closed?"

"Yes."

"Why are your eyes closed?"

I shrugged. "I dunno."

"Don't you think your eyes should be open so you can see your target?"

"But I don't want to see who I'm shooting," was my illogical answer.

He shook his head as if he couldn't believe that I thought that answer made sense. "Chanelle," he began, as if talking to a five-year old. "You have to keep your eyes open when you are shooting a lethal weapon. Can you do that?"

I hated his patronizing tone, so I glared at him. "Yes."

"Good girl. Now do it again. Only this time I want you to look."

"Whatever." I turned to face my target and fired a perfect shot.

He raised his eyebrows. "Wow. I didn't expect that."

I gave him a sassy smirk. "I guess I'm a natural."

"I guess you are."

"Can we leave now?"

"Empty the clip and we can go."

"Bet." I assumed the position and shot four more perfect shots. At least perfect for an amateur. I set the gun down and said, "I'll meet you outside."

I knew Rick was watching me walk out, so I added a little extra sway in my hips. I was happy that my first lesson was successful, but I was petrified at the thought of being in a position to need to shoot somebody.

I stood outside of the front door while I waited for Rick and watched the traffic. Was it my imagination, or was the guy in that navy blue Buick across the street staring at me? Then I felt my phone vibrating in my pocket. I pulled it out and glanced down at the number. I didn't recognize it, so I glanced back to the man in the car. He waved his cell phone in the air and then put it to his ear. I clicked the answer button. "Yes?"

"So you think owning a gun will prepare you for me? My client wants you handled. And I always finish my job."

I didn't respond. Everything around me faded into the background, as I ran across the street toward the car. I didn't hear the horns honking at me. My only focus on was the man who wanted to destroy my life. Destroy me. "Who are you? Who are you? What do you want with me?" I screamed.

Just as I got close to the car, he hit the gas and sped off. All I had time to do was bang his trunk. "What did I do? What did I do? What did I do?" I shouted repeatedly. "Please tell me what I did! Please, please tell me what I did!"

"Chanelle! Chanelle!" Rick yelled my name, as he ran toward me.

I was shaking like a leaf on a windy day, as I pointed in the direction of the now vanished car. "That was him! That was the man! He was right here! Watching me. Oh, my God. Rick, what kind of psycho follows a person to a gun range!"

"Why would you chase after him? Have you lost your mind!" he chastised me, pulling me out of the street and taking me to the safety of the sidewalk.

"It was just a reaction. I wasn't thinking."

"He could have killed you!"

I wailed. "Don't yell at me! Don't you think I know that?"

Rick got his temper under control. "I'm sorry. I'm sorry. I shouldn't have yelled, but he could have seriously hurt you, Chanelle." He held me and stroked my hair, trying to get me to settle down.

"He was here, Rick!" I sobbed into his shirt. "He doesn't care that you're with me. He's waiting for an opportunity to strike. And I have no idea why." I sobbed harder.

"Shhh," he whispered into my hair and continued to hold me. "Let me get you out of here."

I sniffed several times and nodded, as he led me to his truck and took me home.

Chapter 19

"Chanelle, Honey?" I heard a soft voice. But I didn't answer.

I was lying in my bed, staring straight up at the ceiling. I had no idea how long I had been like that. All I knew was that I was never leaving my bedroom again. And no one was going to force me. If I had stayed in my bed earlier, then The Stalker wouldn't have followed me. Although, for all I knew, he was outside my window right now.

"Chanelle?" the voice repeated my name. I finally turned my eyes in the direction of the voice.

"Hi," I muttered.

Michele took that as an invitation to sit on the edge of my bed. "I called your cell and Rick answered. He told me about what happened this afternoon."

"Is he downstairs?"

"He had to make a couple runs, so I told him I'd stay with you while he was gone. He also told me that when he brought you home, you barricaded yourself in here and said you were never coming out."

I moaned. "I'm not. What's the point? To make myself an easier target?"

"We really need to call the police."

I shot straight up in my bed. "We can't. Think about Rachel and my sister. My parents. What about you and Ben and BJ? How do I know that he doesn't know stuff about you? No. No police. Period."

She ignored me. "I have someone here that I want you to talk to." She stood and opened my bedroom door and standing just outside the doorframe was her brother, Steve.

"Hey, Chanelle, what's going on?" he said, entering my room.

I glared at Michele as she sat back on my bed. "I don't care if you're angry with me," she said. "This is serious. And someone who can help needs to know what's going on."

I thought for a moment before I asked, "Steve, are you obligated to report anything I say to you?"

He waited a beat before he spoke. "Let's just say, I'm here as family who happens to have knowledge of the law. And I'm not here as a cop taking your statement."

"So… does that mean that what we talk about stays between us?"

"It means that if I have to escalate it, I'll tell you first."

"Now you sound like your sister," I said, still smarting from the ambush.

"Can you think of anyone who might want to harm you? Have you met anyone new lately?" Steve asked.

I let out a deep breath and slumped against my headboard. "Just Rick. And I know it's not him. Other than that, my last dates were months ago."

Steve sat in my chair across from my bed. "Michele said you received some flowers. Do you know who sent them?"

"Like I told her, I don't."

"Steve," she said to her brother, "do you think this stalking and the flowers are related?"

He nodded. "There's a good chance they are. It could be someone who's jealous about the flowers and obviously wants to send you a message. When you were dating, were you involved in any kind of love triangles?"

"I, uh, accidently ended up in a couple messy situations. My ex has a new lover who was angry with me and sued me, but I thought that was over."

"Are you talking about Michael?"

"Yes. Michael's new boyfriend sued me. But that was so long ago. Although, come to think of it, Michael did email me the other day."

"What did he say?"

"Just that maybe he'd made a mistake and could we talk. I deleted it though and never responded."

"Did he contact you again?"

"Nope."

"Is there anyone else?"

"Well, there was one guy I had one date with that lasted less than 5 minutes, but his girlfriend thought it was more to it and she threatened me. But I didn't take her seriously."

"Have you heard from him recently?"

"Kinda. Chele and I saw him earlier this week. But I tell you, all of my interactions with him totaled less than 10 minutes, and he knows I'm not interested at all. It would be ludicrous to think he's the reason I'm experiencing this.

"Is there anyone else?"

I hesitated as I thought about what to tell him about Sean. "Well…I briefly had a sexual relationship with a guy who had something else with some woman and she was a little obsessed with him. She and I exchanged words. But that was months ago and he doesn't even live here anymore." It was embarrassing enough to tell him that all I had with Sean was sex. I wasn't about to tell him that he had a wife. Michele knew what I was doing, but she didn't call me out.

"Do you think any of these situations could be the cause of what's going on right now?" he asked.

I sighed and shook my head again. "I don't think so. That's why I say I'm at a loss over this."

He stood. "Well, give it some more thought and let me know if anything comes to mind."

I nodded. "I will. And you aren't making this an official discussion, right?"

He looked from me to Michele and back to me. "Not at this time. But you need to be very careful, Chanelle. This person, whoever it is, is serious. And if they contact you again, then I will take official action. One, because it's my duty. And two, because you're as much my sister as Michele is. I wouldn't forgive myself if something happened to you. I'll stay here until Rick gets back." He bent down and kissed me on my forehead. "None of us are going to let anything happen to you."

I felt a sense of relief, knowing that I had so much support. "Thank you."

He tussled his sister's hair and then went downstairs.

"Are you mad at me?" Michele asked.

"Nah. I was expecting it after what happened today. Thanks for not saying anything about Sean's wife."

"Do you think it could be her?"

"I doubt it. Sean said he wasn't going to say anything to her, so how would she know? And you know it didn't come from me. And what happened between us was almost a year ago, so why would she wait until now?" I shook my head. "But, I guess at this point, anything's possible."

The melody of the water flowing down the side of my slate fountain soothed my frayed and frazzled nerves. After several minutes I said, "Michele, I love you. You are my best friend in the entire world. And I know you want what's best for me. But I really need to be alone. I don't feel like talking. I'm a mess on the inside and out and I just want to go to sleep. Tomorrow is a new day and maybe I'll be able to think better. Or maybe I won't leave my room. Either way, it's my choice and right now I choose to be by myself."

Michele stood up and touched my shoulder, then gently kissed the top of my forehead, just as Steve had done. "You are my best friend. And I'm not leaving you alone." She went inside my closet and emerged seconds later with an oversized down blanket and pillow. She walked over to the couch on the far side of my room and made a pallet. "We're in this together. Sleep tight," she said as she laid down for the night.

I reached over and turned off my lamp. In the shadows, she never saw my appreciative smile as I drifted off to sleep.

Chapter 20

"Knock. Knock," Ben said, holding a pizza box in one hand and a 2 liter of Pepsi in the other. Michele was right behind him with plates and cups.

My face lit up. "Oooh, pizza. Yummy. What brings you by?"

"Michele said you refused to leave your room," he said, as he set the box down on the dresser. "So we thought we'd come to you and hang out for awhile."

"You guys are the best. But I've only been locked in here for two days. It's not like I've been hiding out forever." I sat cross-legged on my bed and held out my hands to accept the ooey-gooey goodness from Michele.

"Yeah, but what are you gonna do? Just wait here until the boogey man comes and gets you?" Michele said, sitting on my bed and taking a drink of her soda.

"Of course not. Don't be silly."

"You sure about that? Because hiding yourself in your room is not going to work forever."

"I don't expect it to. I'm just thinking about my options."

She pursed her lips and said, "Mm-hmm. When was the last time you heard from him?"

I glanced away from her, knowing that she'd be able to see through me. "Not since the incident at the gun range."

"Truth or lie?"

"That's something I only do with Andrea."

"Well, you're doing it with me today. Truth or lie?"

"Okay, fine. I may have received a call or two." There was no way I was telling her that he'd called me at least six times, with each call sounding the same. Threats on my life and my family, but never giving a me a clue to the reason or who was paying him.

"Chanelle! Why didn't you say something?"

"So you and your brother could call in the calvary? Nope. I already told you. I'm handling this myself."

"Did you tell Rick?" Ben interjected.

"Um…"

"That would be a 'no'," Michele said, speaking for me.

"I didn't want to stress Rick out."

"Stress me out about what?" he said from the doorway.

"Hey, I didn't hear you come in," I said, my face lighting up.

"Stress me out about what?" he repeated.

"Chanelle received calls from her friend that she didn't tell anyone about."

"You know, Michele, you can quit speaking for me."

Rick looked at me. "When did he call?"

"Yesterday and he didn't say anything he hadn't said before. So what was the point in mentioning it?"

"How did he call and I not know about it?"

I hung my head. "I put my phone on vibrate and kept it under my bedspread."

Everyone looked at me with pure irritation and I felt like I was being scolded by my parents, which put me on the defense.

"Look, this is my life. My drama. I'll handle it in a way that I think is best."

"Snippy, snippy."

"Whatever, Michele. I'm serious. Everyone needs to stop treating me like I don't know how to handle my business."

"And you call locking yourself in your room, handling your business?" she said.

"At this moment, yes I do. Now can we please enjoy a nice meal of junk food and talk about something else?" I rolled my eyes at everyone and dared them to continue the current conversation.

Ben turned to Rick. "I got to give it up to you, man. You have your hands full with this one," he said, pointing to me.

"It's all good. I'm not letting anything happen to her," Rick said, taking a seat next to me on the bed and reaching for a pepperoni off my slice of pizza.

"You're a good dude," Ben said.

I looked at Rick and felt my heart melt like ice cream in a desert. We'd only been back in each other's lives for about a couple weeks, but with what we were going through together, I felt connected to him. Knowing that Ben approved of him helped me settle into our growing friendship.

The trio of wardens allowed me to change the conversation and we talked about lighter topics for the rest of evening. I was thankful to have all of their support, but they were right. I couldn't hide forever. Eventually, I was going to have to figure out my next move. And at the present time, I had no clue what that was going to be.

Chapter 21

A few more days had passed and I was pretty sure that Rick was not going to let me spend one more day in my room, so I mentally started preparing myself to re-enter the world and finally face this issue.

"Chanelle?" he called my name from the other side of my closed door.

"Yes?"

"Are you leaving your room today?" Rick asked.

"I was thinking about it," I said, sitting up in bed and flipping through TV channels.

"I'd love to see you today in something other than mismatched flannel pajamas," he chuckled.

I rolled my eyes, even though he couldn't see me. "Whatever."

Rick cracked the door and peeked in. "And maybe, just maybe you might want to take a shower."

With that, I let out a loud laugh. "I can't stand you!" I exclaimed, hurling a pillow at him.

Laughing with me, he quickly closed the door. "I'm glad you have your spirit back." I heard his footsteps move farther away from my door, as he retreated back down the stairs.

Heading toward my master bath, I was grinning like I'd won the daily lottery. I hated what was going on, but I loved having Rick in my house. I was still smiling after my shower. It had been days since Rick saw me in something presentable and I needed to look and feel attractive.

In my closet, I chose a denim wrap dress with the tags still hanging on it and a new pair of platform sandals. I completed the outfit with a colorful chunky necklace. I quickly applied my makeup and styled my hair in a casual ponytail. I took one final glance in my full-length mirror. Perfect.

"Well, well, well. You look fantastic, Chanelle." Rick said, eyeing me when I walked into the family room.

I gave him a subtle smile as I sat on the couch. "Thank you. And thank you for coaxing me out of my room."

"Any time," he said, continuing to stare at me.

There was so much electricity between us that I started to feel uncomfortable. "Um, you've been my babysitter for awhile now. Are you ever planning to go back to work?

Sensing my discomfort, he looked away and turned his attention to the television. "Max has everything under control so I can keep my schedule clear for you. And I was thinking that maybe we could go out for breakfast and..."

I raised my eyebrow. "And what?"

He turned back to me. "And go back to the gun range." He quickly put up his hand to stop my protest. "I know what happened last time. But this is something that you need to learn how to do. And you learn with practice. Plus, I'll be there with you. So I signed you up for a CPL class. They will perform your background check while we're there and when you leave, you will be licensed to carry a gun."

I closed my eyes as I massaged my temples and thought about Rick's request. I knew he was right, but what if The Stalker followed us again? For that matter, what if he was outside now? What if he'd been outside my house for days? What if? What if? What if? This madness had to stop! I steeled my nerves. "Okay. Let's do it."

"That's it? No more push back?"

I shook my head. "Nope. You're right. I need to learn to protect myself. I can't expect you to continue to take care of me."

"I enjoy taking care of you, Chanelle."

I smiled at him. "I know you do. And I really appreciate you, Rick. But I need to become independent again. Hiding like a wuss isn't who I am. So if it means that I have to learn how to shoot a gun, then that's what I'm going to do." I paused before adding, "Besides, I like it when we shoot together."

Rick was thrown by my comment, but quickly recovered. "Then, come on, woman! Let's go." He stood and pulled me up with him.

Laughing, I followed him out to the garage and tossed him the keys to my Range Rover. "I feel like taking Gigi today. Do you mind driving?"

"Of course not. Why do you call her Gigi?" he asked, as he opened my door for me before going around to the driver's side and starting the motor.

"It stands for 'God's Gift'. It was something I always wanted and in an impulsive moment, I bought her."

"That's pretty cool. So where do you feel like eating?" he asked.

"I'm flexible. And it's my treat."

"Leo's Coney Island?"

"Works for me," I said as I tuned my audio system to my Kurt Carr playlist. "I hope you're okay with gospel music."

"I love gospel music. Marvin Sapp. Kirk Franklin. Old school Winans."

Hmmm... I thought. The Rick from college days would have never listened to gospel music. But back then, I didn't either.

We drove in silence, enjoying the scenery around us and the inspiration piping from my Bose speakers. When we arrived at Leo's, the hostess led us to a table in the back and told us our waitress would be with us shortly.

"So, when did you start listening to gospel music," I asked.

"A few years back. Max was in a bad car accident and the doctors said there was nothing they could do for him. I used my street money to buy him the best medical treatment I could afford, and it still wasn't good enough. As a last resort, I went to church, and something happened. I can't explain it, but I gave my life to God and started praying for my brother. And God healed him."

"Wow."

"Sorry to keep you waiting," the waitress interrupted us as she approached our table. "Can I get you started with something to drink?"

"Yes, please. I'll have a cup of coffee," I said.

"I'll have the same."

"Two coffees coming up," she said. But not before giving Rick the once over.

I couldn't blame her. There was no denying that he was hot. But she was rude for checking him out in front me since she didn't know if I was his wife or girlfriend. However, since I was neither, I didn't comment.

"What about you? When did you start listening to gospel music?" he asked, returning to our conversation.

"Not long after I left college. My parents have always been big into church. I strayed while I was away at school. Then after I graduated, I guess you could say I returned to my roots."

"Nice. So you've been living a Godly life for a long time then."

"I try. But nobody's perfect," I said, thinking about how I lived with Michael for years and had an affair with Sean. An affair that probably would have continued if he hadn't moved out of town.

"Maybe this Sunday, you and I could go to church together," he suggested.

I studied him. "You've truly changed. I'd love that."

"Then it's a date."

Our waitress returned with our beverages. "Here you go. Two cups of coffee. Are you ready to order?" she asked, looking only at Rick.

"Chanelle, you go first," he volunteered.

"I'll have a veggie omelet with hash browns and turkey bacon."

"Mm-hmm," she said, all but dismissing me. Then looked at Rick again. "And what can I get you, Sweetheart? The Hungry Man special?"

I didn't want Rick to see me show my butt, but I was very close to losing my patience. He ignored her flirtatious tone, and said, "Actually, I'll have the short stack of blueberry pancakes and sausage."

"Got it," she said, flashing more teeth than any one person should have.

When she sauntered away, I said, "You know she was flirting with you, right?"

"I don't pay any attention to women like her. I'm here with you. You're who I want to get to know better. Not some trifling woman who is disrespectful to my date. But I don't want her playing hockey with our food, so I let it go." He chuckled.

I was glad to know that he'd observed what she was doing and he'd intentionally blown her off because of me. "Thank you. I appreciate that."

"One thing you'll learn about me is that I'm a one-woman guy. I was that way when we were together in college. I was that way when I was married. And I'm that way now. Cheating and straying are words that aren't in my vocabulary. And I hope they aren't in your vocabulary."

Not anymore. "No, those words aren't in my vocabulary either."

"I'd be surprised if they were," he said, smiling at me and having no idea that I was becoming increasingly uncomfortable with our conversation.

"Uh, tell me about today. How long do you think we'll be at the gun range?"

He proceeded to tell me how the rest of the day would unfold and after a few moments, I was able to set aside thoughts of our discussion about fidelity. We enjoyed breakfast, and our waitress finally got the hint that he wasn't interested. Thankfully, our food had already arrived before she figured it out.

After breakfast, we headed to the gun range. I gave them the information needed to start my background check, and then Rick rented a 9 millimeter, like the one he owned.

"Why didn't you get a .22 caliber again?" I questioned, as we walked back to the practice area.

"Because I see those as starter guns. I want you to be able to shoot a gun that can do some damage. With a .22, if a guy has on a heavy coat, he might not even feel it."

"Oh, I didn't know that."

"That's why you have me to teach you," he said, winking at me. "We have about an hour before your class starts, and I want you to get comfortable with it." He repeated the lesson he'd given me days earlier, and I felt same charge when he stood behind me. My entire body warmed and I quivered slightly. It was kind of nice to be so attracted to someone who was equally attracted to me. And I was quickly gaining confidence in my ability as a shooter.

Toward the end of our lesson, Rick said, "Okay, now I'm not going to talk you through it and I want you to show me what you've learned."

"Yes, coach." I mimicked the stance I'd been taught and cocked the gun. I closed one eye and when my target came into focus, I pulled the trigger.

Rick pushed the button that brought the target paper to us. I had landed an almost perfect bull's eye. He stared at the paper in amazement and then looked at me.

I was just as shocked as he was, but I just shrugged and played it cool. "I'm a natural shot."

"You have no idea how sexy you are to me right now."

"I think I have an idea," I said, scanning his body and noticing his rise of excitement.

He chuckled and shook his head. "I can't even hide it, and you're definitely ready for your class."

"You're right. You can't hide it. And yes, I'm ready for class," I said, laughing.

The four-hour lesson was a breeze. When we returned our equipment, the clerk said my background check came back clear, handed me a temporary certificate, and informed me that my permanent card would come in the mail.

I was feeling pretty good, but when Rick went to talk to the instructor, I waited inside the building. No way was I standing outside by myself again. He came back and told me the instructor said I was one of the best female students he'd ever seen.

I was definitely on a high as we walked out into the bright daylight. I got into the Rover just as Rick received a phone call and excused himself. When he returned, his brows were furrowed.

"What's wrong?" I asked with concern in my voice, as Rick got into the driver's seat.

He shut the door and pushed the ignition button. "It's nothing major. I have a guy working for me and he ran into a problem on a job that Max can't handle." He turned to me. "I hate to do this to you, Chanelle, but I need to check it out. Do you wanna ride or do you want me to drop you off at home?"

I felt panic come over me. I was petrified to be home alone, but I didn't want to be a tag-along. Besides, I didn't think it would be professional for me to go with him. "I'll be fine at home," I lied.

"Are you sure? Do you want me to call Michele?"

I shook my head. "Thanks, but I'm fine. I have to be comfortable taking care of myself." I placed my hand on top of his and looked him in the eyes. "Go. Handle your business."

Rick hesitated before speaking. "I'll work as quickly as I can."

"I know you will. Now let's go. Okay?"

"Okay." He put the SUV in reverse and backed out of our parking space.

The ride to my house was silent. I didn't want Rick to know how worried I was so I gave myself a mental pep talk, which was clearly not working. As we pulled up in front of my house, my head was going around like a corkscrew. Even though there was no sign of the dark sedan, Rick went inside and checked out every room on every floor. Once satisfied that I was the only one inside, he headed toward the front door. "Make sure you set the alarm."

"Please stop worrying, Rick. You're going to make me nervous. And besides, the sooner you leave, then the sooner you'll be back."

"You're right. I'm sorry. Okay, I'm leaving. My job is about 20 minutes away, but if you need me, call me."

"You are so sweet." I kissed him on the cheek and pushed him out the door. "I'll be here when you get back."

"Promise?"

"I promise."

Closing the door behind him, I prayed that was a promise that I would be able to keep.

Chapter 22

As I watched TV in my den, I heard the distant ring of my home phone, which was in the kitchen. I glanced at the clock and realized Rick had been gone about three hours. Thinking it might be him, I jumped off the couch and raced through my house to the kitchen to answer it before the ringing stopped. Looking at the caller ID, I tensed momentarily. I didn't recognize the number, but it was different from the number The Stalker had been using. Maybe Rick was calling me from another phone. "Hello?" I said tentatively.

"Chanelle?" a male voice asked.

"Who's calling?"

He cleared his throat as though he were nervous. "Uh, Sean. Sean. It's Sean. From work."

"Sean?" I asked incredulously.

"Yes. Is now a good time to talk?"

"Um. I guess so." I was trying to figure out why he was calling me since we hadn't spoken in months.

"How have you been?" he asked.

"Fine. And you?"

He hesitated. "I've been okay. I'm planning a trip to Michigan and I was hoping maybe we could get together for dinner."

"Um. I'm not sure that's such a good idea."

"I understand. But I really want to see you. I have something I need to tell you."

"Can you tell me now?"

"Well, I'd prefer to tell you in person."

I sighed heavily. "Sean, I have a lot going on these days."

"I understand," he repeated himself. "It's just that I've missed you and I need to talk to you."

"I don't want to hurt your feelings and I'm sure you're still a great guy, but I'm not interested in having dinner with you. That moment in my life has passed. I hope you will respect my decision," I said, with more force than I intended.

"Cynthia and I aren't together anymore!" he announced.

"O-K... Well, if you're happy, then I'm happy for you."

"I don't think you're following me. We're not together. So that means you and I have a chance to explore a real relationship."

I pulled the phone away from my ear, staring at it as though it were a foreign object. "Like I said, I'm happy for you, but I have no desire to be with you, Sean. I'm embarrassed by what happened between us and, quite honestly, I want to forget it."

"Did you like the flowers?"

My blood turned to ice. "What did you just ask me?" I said sharply.

"Uh... uh...," he stuttered. "The flowers. I know how much you like yellow roses. And I added some white ones because I wanted you to know that my love for you is pure."

I felt like all the oxygen had left my brain and my room began to spin. I tried to sort out what I had just heard. Slowly I asked, "Are you telling me that you sent me flowers with a card that read 'What if'?"

"Yes. Did you like them?"

Slowly, I asked, "Sean, did you tell Cynthia about us?"

He stalled. "Why do you ask?"

"Because I need to know. Did you tell her?"

"I may have said something about it." Then he quickly added, "But only after I told her that I wanted a divorce."

"Oh my God," I said, collapsing against my granite countertop. I put my head in my hands and took several deep breaths.

Sean said, "I wanted to send you something to show you that I still think about you," he continued.

I closed my eyes. "Sean. Cynthia knows that you sent me flowers."

"Why do you think she knows?"

"I *know* she knows because she sent me a dead rat after you sent those darn flowers."

I could hear his confusion when we asked, "What are you talking about?"

"I got the flowers that you sent, and while I was trying to figure out who they were from, I got a threatening phone call from some man who said he was paid by his client to seek revenge on me for what I did. And then a few days later, I received a dead rat… *at work*." I took a deep breath and continued. "Sean, all this is happening to me because you decided to tell Cynthia something. And I may not know exactly what you told her, but whatever it was, it was enough for her to think I'm the reason her marriage is falling apart!"

"I am so very sorry. I had no idea that she would do something like that."

"What would make you think that I would be okay with flowers from you? I mean seriously, have you lost your mind?" By now I was in full-blown anger mode. "My life has been flipped upside down and turned inside out, and all you can say is you're sorry and you had no idea? Are you nuts? You told me you weren't going to tell her!"

"I wanted to do something nice for you. Telling her just happened."

"Ugh! How are you going to fix this?" I had several emotions running through me. I was thankful to finally know what started all of this, but I was also scared, because of all the options it could have been, Cynthia was the worst possible scenario. She was a woman scorned. And scorned women knew no boundaries. For the first time since this drama began I actually considered calling the cops.

And then I thought about my career. What would happen if I went to the cops and somehow Mr. Jeffries found out? How would he respond if he knew a partner in his firm had an affair with a consultant? Even though it had happened before my promotion, would he fire me for violating the ethics clause in my employment agreement?

And what about Rick? How in the world could I tell him that all this was happening because of an affair I had? What would he think of me? Would he be able to see beyond it or would he judge me based on one indiscretion? Well, two indiscretions. I wondered if our relationship was too new to survive something like this.

The sound of Sean's voice snapped me out of my thoughts. "Chanelle, I'll talk to Cynthia and find out what she did."

"Thanks. But more importantly, I need you to call her off me."

"How do you expect me to do that?"

"I have no idea, but you better do something. Tell her that you changed your mind about the divorce."

"But I haven't. Cynthia changed when we moved to Virginia. She never connected with an AA group and she's been going downhill. She's even in jeopardy of losing her veterinarian license because of things she's done recently."

I disregarded him and said, "I need you to at least try. Do you realize that I have been living in fear for my life since you sent me those dumb flowers? I haven't been able to work. I barely eat, sleep, or leave my house. Heck, it's hard for me to leave my bedroom. And this is your mess. Now clean it up!"

"I'll see what I can do." He stammered before saying, "Does this mean that I won't be able to see you when I get to Michigan?"

I rubbed my forehead. Was this fool for real? I swear his IQ dropped when he moved to Virginia. "You are correct. The next time I hear from you, you better be tellin' me that you have Cynthia under control."

Sean sounded dejected and said, "I understand, Chanelle. I also need to tell you that the reason I'm coming to Michigan is because I'm interviewing to get my job back at Image."

All the air instantly left the room. "You're what?"

"I'm moving back to Michigan if Image has a spot for me."

"Oh." This was getting worse by the moment.

"Anyway, I'll be in touch."

And with that, I disconnected the phone call.

Chapter 23

It had been close to an hour since I hung up with Sean, but it felt like five minutes. As I slumped against the kitchen counter, trying to figure out what to do next, the phone in my hand rang. I hadn't realized that I'd never set it back in the cradle. I checked the caller ID.

"Boy, am I glad you called me!" I said to Andrea the moment I answered the phone. "I have so much to tell you!"

"And hello to you, too." Andrea said. "But I called because I need a favor."

"It'll have to wait because right now I need my sister. Can you come over?"

Andrea changed her tone and became serious. "What's goin' on, lil sis?"

"I'll tell you when you get here."

"I'm on my way."

I was thankful to spend some time with my sister. We didn't talk often because about the only thing we had in common was blood. But that blood was enough. We had a lot of love for each and Andrea was the perfect person to talk to about what was going on now. She might not have a solution, but she'd be a good sounding board.

I set the phone back in its cradle and I went into my main floor bathroom to splash cold water on my face, and then back to the kitchen to prepare a snack. I didn't really have an appetite, but I knew I needed to put something in my stomach. I settled on a platter of cheeses, crackers, grapes, strawberries, and a bottle of Riesling. I was carrying the goodies into the den when I heard my front door open. My heart stopped until I remembered that Andrea had the alarm code and a key to my house.

"It's just me!" she called out.

"I'm in here!" I responded. "How'd you get here so fast?"

"I was around the corner. So what's up?" she said, walking into the den and sitting on the couch. "What's with the bougie food? You ain't got no wings?"

"Andrea, I'm going to need you to focus on me for a change. Now have a drink. You'll need it because you won't believe me when I tell you what's been going on." I proceeded to fill my sister in on the last several months of my life, starting with Sean.

"You gotta be kiddin' me," she said when I finished speaking.

"I wish."

"You was kickin' it with some married dude? That don't even sound like you."

"What can I say? I got caught up. And now I'm paying for it."

"So what you goin' do?"

"I dunno," I said, while I popped a grape into my mouth.

"You tellin' Rick?"

"Which part? The affair? I know who's stalking me? Sean may be moving back?"

"All of it."

"I don't know yet. What do you think I should do? Everyone is telling me to call the cops."

"Girl, you don't need no cops."

"You don't think so?"

"Nah. We got the same blood. If I wouldn't need no cops, then you don't need no cops," she said, then continued. "But you can't keep hidin' in your room like some little bi-"

"Don't say it," I cut her off. "But I hear you. I'll handle it."

Andrea rolled her neck. "You sure?"

"I said I'll handle it."

"Let me know if you need help. And if he comes near my daughter, I'll take him out myself."

That's why I loved my sister. I could always count on her to have my back. "Thanks, Sis."

"So you and Rick are kickin' it again?"

I blushed. "I don't know what we're doing. But he's been amazing to me since this whole ordeal began. We've gotten very close in a short amount of time."

"That's cool. But if we done talkin' about you, I need to get to that favor."

I shook my head. "You listened to me longer than I thought you would. What do you need?"

"I need you to let me hold a few hundred. And before you say no, it's for Rachel."

"What does she need?"

"She wanna take swimming lessons and I ain't got no money for 'em."

"Wait here." I ran upstairs to my bedroom and reached inside my jewelry box on my dresser. I returned moments later with the bracelet from Sean. "Here. Pawn this and keep the money." I handed her the unpleasant reminder of the mistakes of my past.

"Straight up? You givin' me this?"

"Yeah. Take it before I change my mind. And I can't think about this anymore today. I'm sure Rick will be here soon and I don't want to have this on my mind when he arrives."

"Don't want to have what on your mind?"

I quickly turned in the direction of the voice. "Oh! You have to stop appearing out of nowhere! You almost gave me a heart attack!" I said, clutching my chest and praying that my heartbeat would return to normal. How long had he been standing there?

"I'm sorry, Chanelle. I thought you heard me. I announced myself when I came in. So what don't you want to have on your mind?" he questioned me again.

"Just this whole nightmare." My response was the truth. I was too consumed with this and I had to find a way to let it go.

But now I felt guilty when I looked at Rick. He had so much concern in his face that I wanted to confess to everything right then and there. "Rick, I have something I need to tell you."

But Andrea cut me off. "Hey, Rick, it's good to see you again."

"You too, Andrea. You're still lookin' good. Beauty must run in your family." He hugged her, then turned back to me. "What is it that you need to say?"

"It'll have to wait," she interrupted again. "I'm gettin' ready to go. Sis, walk me to my car, okay?"

I frowned, unsure of what she was up to. I turned to Rick. "I'll be back in a minute."

I followed my sister through the house and out the front door to her car with tape over the taillights. "Why did you stop me?" I said.

"Because you was 'bout to screw up a good thing. It took me two seconds to see that he is really checking for you. You tell him what you did with ol' boy, and poof," she snapped her fingers, "just like that, Rick will be gone."

"You think so?"

"Sis, I know so. Keep yo mouth shut and take care of yo business."

I contemplated what Andrea was telling me. Was she right? I thought talking to her would help me sort things out, but instead I was more confused than ever.

"What am I supposed to say when I go back inside?"

"I dunno." She shrugged. "You'll come up with somethin' good," she said, kissing me on my cheek. "I gotta go. Call me if you need me."

I smirked. "Thanks."

I watched my sister drive off, wishing I was in the passenger seat, then realized I was standing outside alone and sprinted back into the house. Andrea was right. I had it in me to take care of this myself. I couldn't risk losing Rick. We were building a solid foundation for a lasting relationship. And it was finally within reach. There was no way I was going to jeopardize it.

"Is Andrea okay?" Rick asked when I returned to the den.

"Yeah. She's the same as she was when you knew her before. She was just keeping me company while you were gone."

"So what was it that you wanted to tell me?"

"Um… it was nothing serious. Just that I missed you and couldn't wait for you to get home." I looked up at him through my lashes and twirled my hair around my finger. "I'm scared when you're not here."

His voice was soft when he said, "It'll be over soon. I promise you, I'll find out who's doing this to you and make them pay."

"That's why you're my protector. Would you like a glass of wine?" I asked, while pouring myself my second glass of the evening. And then, downing it in two gulps.

"Nah, I'm good. But you need to slow down. It's wine, not water."

"I know. But I need something to take the edge off," I said as I quickly poured and drank my third glass.

"That's it. You're cut off." Rick grabbed the bottle and my empty wine glass, while I wiped my mouth on the back of my sleeve. "Would you like me to fix you dinner?"

"Oh, no. I couldn't ask you to do that. You just finished working. I'm sure you must be tired."

"You didn't ask. I volunteered. And I don't mind. I'll do a quick check around the house and we can fire up the grill."

"But the grill is outside."

"That's usually where people keep them. No one is going to hurt you while I'm around."

I smiled at my guardian angel. "Then barbecue would be great. I think I have a pack of Amish chicken wings in the refrigerator. I'll whip up a quick marinade, while you start the grill. There's a big bag of lump charcoal in the garage."

"Perfect," Rick said and headed to the kitchen to drop off the glasses and the remaining wine before heading to the garage. I stood up and wobbled a little, but quickly caught my balance and followed him into the kitchen. Once he left, I poured and gulped my fourth glass of wine, then created a teriyaki marinade for the chicken.

Dinner was pretty good. He fixed chicken and grilled asparagus, and for dessert, he grilled slices of pineapple. I was extra chatty, thanks to the wine. He was a gentleman and pretended not to notice.

After dinner, Rick grabbed the dirty dishes. "You rest while I clean up."

I just stared at him. I was so grateful to him and thankful to God that he had re-entered my life.

I leaned back into my lounger and closed my eyes. My thoughts were jumbled and I wanted to be me again. This ordeal had consumed my life. I needed to get away. For a fleeting moment, I thought about leaving the country. Maybe The Stalker didn't have a passport. I chuckled to myself.

"It's nice to see you smile." I opened my eyes to see Rick smiling down at me.

"It feels good to smile."

Rick had turned on my stereo system and the sounds of R. Kelly's latest hits filled the room.

"Let's dance," he said, extending his hand to me.

I didn't hesitate. He pulled me up and tenderly took me in his arms. We swayed to the smooth rhythm. I rested my head on his chest and again closed my eyes. I inhaled deeply and took in the scent of his woodsy cologne. The cascade of the water flowing from my fountain, combined with the melodic tunes, and the safety of a strong man's arms were so comforting. For the first time that day, I felt all the tension leave my body. I knew I had decisions to make, but for now, I was going to enjoy the moment. And pretend that all was perfect in my world.

I looked up at Rick. "Thank you."

"For what?" he asked.

"For being such a friend to me. I don't know how I would have made it without you."

He tightened his grip on me. "Thank you for trusting me enough to protect you." He placed his finger under my chin and tilted my head up as he bent down to give me the sweetest kiss I'd ever experienced in my 30 plus years of living. His lips were so soft that I felt my body melt into his.

I grabbed his head as he pulled me even closer and our kiss deepened.

"Chanelle?" Rick said my name in a voice filled with undeniable desire.

"Yes?"

"I want to make love to you."

My heart fluttered. "I—I would like that. But it's too soon."

"I'll wait as long as I have to. I knew that I still loved you when I saw you in Lowe's. I'm in this with you for the long haul. I'll wait as long as it takes for you to trust that I'm not going to hurt you and that I'm not going anywhere."

I prayed that he was being honest with me because I knew that I could love him, too. But it was just too early in our relationship. Even Steve Harvey said women should wait at least 90 days. So I pushed away a little. "Rick, I just need more time. I'm emotional right now and a little tipsy," I added with a light laugh. "When we make love, I want my head to be clear."

"Okay. Like I said, I can wait as long as it takes."

"Thank you," I said softly as a lone tear slid down my cheek.

He gently kissed it away. Then he kissed my closed eyelids, my cheeks, my nose, and finally my mouth. Our kiss intensified and I was about five seconds from changing my mind.

"We need to stop before we go farther than we should," I said as I tried to compose myself.

"You're right," he said with his mouth, but his eyes were pleading with me to keep it going.

I listened to his mouth. "I'm going to bed and I'm sleeping alone." I paused before adding, "Tonight."

"Does that mean that maybe you won't be sleeping alone tomorrow?"

I smiled coyly and shrugged one shoulder. "I dunno about tomorrow. I guess you'll have to wait and see." I leaned in and kissed him on his cheek. "Good night, Rick," I said and headed out of the room.

I felt him staring at my backside. "Good night, Chanelle. I love you."

I stopped walking and turned to face him.

"Too much?" he asked.

I nodded. "Yes, too much."

"Okay. Then just good night."

I smiled and left the room.

Chapter 24

"Hey, Boss Lady, How are things going?" Patty asked when she called my house.

"Things are fine. How's work?" I said, while sitting in my living room, reading a novel by one of my favorite authors.

"We miss you. People are asking about you."

"What are you telling them?"

"That you're on an extended vacation. Mr. Jeffries is the only one who knows that you are on a leave of absence. Do you have any idea when you'll be back?"

"That's a great question and I have no answer." It had been a couple days since my call with Sean. I hadn't heard anything from The Stalker since we spoke, so maybe he was able to get through to his wife.

"Well, I have good news for you."

"Please share. I could use some good news."

"Sean may be coming back."

That wasn't good news. "Oh."

"Yeah, Mr. Jeffries told me yesterday. He's pumped about it. I guess Sean called and told him that he was returning to

Michigan and asked about getting his consultant spot back. Mr. Jeffries said he would hire him back in a New York minute."

"And Mr. Jeffries just volunteered that information?"

"Yeah. That's how excited he was. He came by to tell you and then remembered that you were out. So he told me."

Breathe, Chanelle, breathe. "Well, I hope things work out."

"Aren't you happy about this, Boss Lady? You and Sean were like the dynamic duo."

"I'm happy. Look I have to go. But thanks for telling me," I said, rushing her off the phone.

"Oh, okay. I'll talk to you later."

After hanging up with Patty, I stared out my bay window and thought about the travesty that was unfolding before my very eyes. My life was becoming exponentially worse.

Through my window, I noticed a white Impala driving at a snail's crawl down my block. The driver paced the street twice before coming to a stop in front of my house. I leaned forward in my chair to get a closer look inside the car and I could swear that the driver was Cynthia. She had on sunglasses and a scarf around her head, and when she raised her glasses and our eyes locked, I confirmed that it was her. We stared at each other for several seconds before she tipped up a bottle that looked like it could have been whiskey, and sped off.

I could hear Michele's voice in my head telling me to call the police. But what would I say? I didn't think it was a crime. It was just creepy. But there was one person I could call.

"Hey, Steve, it's your other sister," I said, the moment he answered.

"What's going on, Chanelle? Are you alright?"

"Yeah, I'm fine. I just, I just…"

"What? Spit it out."

"I think I saw a woman in front of my house who may be connected with the stalking."

"What makes you think that? And can you describe her?"

"Um…" What was I going to say? Of course I could describe her, but I hadn't told him about Cynthia. Now I could hear Andrea's voice in my head telling me to man up and leave Steve out of it.

"Chanelle? Are you still there?"

"Yeah, I'm here. Uh, it was a false alarm. I—I missed the pizza sign on top of the car. It must have been a delivery person looking for an address."

"Mm-hmm. Are you sure?" he asked.

"I'm positive. I was just being jumpy. Sorry to have bothered you. I'll call you if I need you."

I hung up before he could continue the conversation.

Okay, Sherlock, I said to myself. Now what are you going to do?

"Chanelle, dinner was delicious. You keep cooking like this and I'm never leaving," Rick said, savoring the final bites of his smothered pork chops, collard greens, and rice.

"Is that a promise?" I smiled at him from across the table.

"It could be."

My heart skipped and I took a sip of my wine, trying to calm the ripples in my stomach. "You ready for dessert? I fixed an apple pie."

"What I'm ready for is a conversation about us."

I glanced away and he reached across the mahogany wood and caressed my fingers, sending yet another tremor through my body. "I'm ready to talk about us. I want there to be an 'us', don't you?"

I looked at his hands, then allowed my eyes to travel up his arms, stopping momentarily at his ripped chest and finally to his handsome face. "Yes, I want there to be an 'us'."

"Just you and me. I don't have a desire to date anyone but you."

I wanted to move forward and tell him I wanted the exact same thing, because honest to God, I did. I wanted to be with Rick and only Rick. But I couldn't do it until I'd resolved my Sean/Cynthia issues. "I… I can't really focus on a relationship right now. Not until I get my life straightened out. Can you understand where I'm coming from?"

He slid his hands back to his side of the table and his lips turned down, but he nodded. "Yeah. Yeah, I can understand."

"Um, I'll get dessert. Why don't you relax and I'll bring it to you." Slowly, we stood. He went into the den without speaking another word, and I grabbed our plates, went into the kitchen, and sliced the pie and scooped vanilla ice cream.

"Here you go," I said, meeting him in the den and handing him his bowl while sitting next to him on the love seat.

The mood was noticeably awkward, but I didn't know what to say. So I said nothing and prayed he'd get over it and go back to being the Rick I enjoyed, instead of the one I'd just hurt. After about 20 minutes of being bored as I could be watching the Military Channel, which was his favorite, the cordless phone rang. I tensed when I picked it up and saw "unknown" on the caller ID. I peeked at Rick before I put the phone to the side of my face that was farthest from him and said, "Hello?"

"Hi, Chanelle. It's me, Sean."

I pressed the phone closer to my ear, and subtly turned down the volume on the side of the receiver. "Oh, hey," I said, glancing again at Rick, who was watching me intently.

"Is now a good time to talk?"

"Uh, not really."

Rick mouthed, "Is that him?"

I shook my head and looked away, trying to figure out what I was going to tell him when I hung up.

"Okay, well, I was just calling to let you know that I haven't been able to talk to Cynthia about you. She's not speaking to me. She moved out and changed her phone number when I told her I got the job at Image."

He dealt me a double whammy. My hopes of having him call her off plummeted and my anxiety about him returning shot through the proverbial roof.

"Did you hear me?" he continued.

"Yeah. Thanks for letting me know."

"I'll see you soon, Chanelle. And I'm not giving up on us. We could have something very special if you just give us a chance."

"Thanks again for calling. I'll be sure to keep that in mind."

"Huh?"

"Gotta go now. Bye."

"Who was that?" Rick asked immediately after I hung up.

"Just the office. Patty was giving me a quick update. No big deal," I said, chewing on my bottom lip.

Rick peered at me out of the corner of his eye, as if trying to decide whether or not he should believe me. "You know, when we were in college, I could always tell when you weren't being straight with me."

I scrunched my eyebrows. "What are you talking about?"

"Whenever, you told a half truth or you out and out lied, you would bite your lip… sorta like what you're doing now."

I promptly stopped. "I'm being straight with you. It was work."

"Mm-hmm." He turned his attention back to the television, but I knew he wasn't watching. He was trying to guess what I was up to. And I was trying to figure out how I was going to balance my disastrous life.

Chapter 25

"Hey, can you come over?" I said to my best friend over the phone, the morning after finding out that Sean was definitely returning.

"Sure. What time?"

"Whenever's good for you. Rick left for work I just don't want to be home alone. So I was hoping we could have a little girl time."

"Well, aren't you the little housewife. Seems like you're never going back to work."

I giggled. "I have to admit, I could get used to this kind of life. You know, minus the stalker part."

"I'm glad to know you can joke about it," she said. "I'll swing by after I drop BJ off at preschool."

"Okay. Thanks."

We hung up and I called my sister. "Hey, can you come over?"

"What you want?"

"Why can't you just say, 'yes, my favorite baby sister, I'm on my way'?"

"Because I don't roll like that. But since you did me a solid when you gave me that tennis bracelet, I'll leave out in about 30 minutes."

"Thank you. Love you."

"Yeah yeah yeah," she said, then hung up.

I rolled my eyes at my sister's response, then said my daily prayer to God, took a shower, quickly dressed, and headed downstairs to start my day. I was enjoying a cup of tea and a bowl of oatmeal when my phone rang. I hated that I felt compelled to answer when I was sure I didn't want to talk to whoever was on the other end of the line. But without fail, I said, "Hello."

"Humph. So you think you can ruin my marriage and den go on like nothin' happened, huh?"

I frowned. "Cynthia?"

"Who else would be it be? Who else's marriage did you jack up?" she snarled.

I ignored her biting words. "Cynthia, I'm sorry that your marriage is ruined, as you say. But I didn't do that." I shook my head as though she could see me.

"Ha! Yeah, you did," she slurred.

I remained calm. Maybe if I could just reason with her, she would leave me alone and go on about her life. "Cynthia, I truly apologize to you if I hurt you in anyway. What happened between Sean and me was a mistake. And will never happen again."

"You right it was a mistake," she snarled. "Because of you he's leaving me."

"I don't know why you say that. Sean and I haven't spoken since you moved." My comment wasn't completely true, but it wasn't like I wanted to talk to him when he called.

"He moved all right, but he wasn't the same. He kept talkin' 'bout how he wanted to get back to Michigan and I couldn't understand why. And den one day, he comes home from church and he's feelin' all guilty and he start tellin' me 'bout you. And how he misses you. And how he don't wanna be married to me no more because he wanna try and make it work wit you." Every time she emphasized "you," her voice escalated.

I was floored, but apparently there was no need for me to speak because she kept talking. "So den I said to myself, 'self, if we got rid of her, den Sean will stay wit us'. And me and myself liked dat idea. So guess what? I'm 'bout to get rid of you."

"Cynthia," I said sternly as I moved to the living room, crouched down on the floor, and looked closely out the window through the curtains. I saw Cynthia parked in a silver Impala in front of my house, but this time she didn't see me. Fortunately, her car was pulled up far enough for me to get a good view of the license plate.

Staying low to the ground, I opened the desk drawer next to the recliner and grabbed a pen and piece of paper. "I told you I was sorry for what I did," I said, cradling the phone in the crook of my neck and jotting down her license plate. "And I feel bad for you because your marriage is on the rocks. But that's not my fault. That's between you and Sean. And if you come at me, I will defend myself." I paused before adding. "I'm not afraid of you." I knew that part was a complete and total lie, but she didn't.

"You shouldn't be afraid. You should be terrified. I'll be in touch." And with that, she hung up and sped off. I remained still as a statue for a few moments, while I tried to process what had just happened.

I returned the pen and paper to the drawer, and resolved right then and there that this nonsense had to end. Now.

Chapter 26

"She was actually outside your house?" Michele asked when I told her and Andrea about my interaction with Cynthia.

I nodded. "Yup. That's the second time that I know of that she's been here."

"Why didn't you tell me sooner?"

"So you could call Steve? No thank you."

"Why would you bring Steve into this?" Andrea spoke up.

"Why wouldn't she?" Michele asked.

"She wouldn't because she can handle some drunk veterinarian with a grudge," she said to Michele, then turned to me. "You're a punk if you bring in the cops."

"Look, I didn't call you two over here for that. I called you to tell you that Sean is definitely returning."

"What?" they said in unison.

"You heard me. Sean is moving back to Michigan. And he got his job back as our consultant. *And* he wants us to pick up where we left off."

"You might as well quit now," Andrea said. "Because this is messy."

"Who you tellin'? But there's no way I'm giving up my job. I've worked to hard to build my career to watch it vanish."

Michele said, "Your career is worthless if you're dead."

I glared at her. I was beginning to wish I hadn't called either one of them. "You're not being helpful, Michele."

"Just calling it the way I see it. But anyway, what about Rick? Have you told him anything about Sean?"

I shook my head. "Last night, he told me he wants to be exclusive. And then later in the evening, Sean called. While I was sitting next to Rick."

"Oooh, what you do?" Andrea asked.

"I pretended like I was on the phone with work."

"Did he buy it?"

I shook my head. "I don't think so. But he let it go."

"Chanelle, you can't build a relationship on lies. It'll kill it before it starts."

"I know that, Michele. But what was I gonna say?"

"Here's a novel idea. How about you tell him the truth?"

"Yeah, right. 'Hey, Rick. I know you think I'm a sweet girl and all, but I slept with a married man and by the way, we'll be working together again really soon. You still wanna be my boyfriend?' Is that how it's supposed to go?"

"See, Sis, that's why I told you to handle yo business by yourself. Because ain't no man stickin' with you if you tell him that."

"Chanelle," Michele began, pulling me out of my gloomy thoughts. "If you keep being secretive, then it's gonna blow up in your face. You have to tell Rick. You can handle everything else that's happening if you start with talking to him. He'll understand. It's not like you two were together when you slept with Sean. But what he won't understand, is you intentionally deceiving him. Don't make a bad situation worse. I'm just sayin'…"

The three of us continued to talk about my problems and eventually gravitated to other topics. But in the back of my mind, I kept replaying Michele's warning. "Don't make a bad situation worse." And that was exactly what I was doing.

"Hey, Sweetie, come on downstairs. I have a surprise for you," Rick yelled up.

It had been a couple hours since the ladies had left and after some soul searching, I decided to come clean to Rick. And deal with whatever happened next. Hopefully, he wouldn't pack his bags. But if he did, then I had only myself to blame.

I took a deep breath, dragged myself off my bed, and went downstairs.

He smiled when he saw me and then came to me with his arms wide open. I walked into them and allowed his warm embrace to comfort me. "The pizza will be here in about 20 minutes," he said as he released me, took my hand and led me to the couch. "I'll be right back. Let me make you some tea. And then I'll give you your surprise."

I gave him a weak smile as I sat. I have a surprise for him too, I thought. Moments later he returned with a cup of steaming hot chamomile tea with organic honey, lemon, and ginger. It was delicious and just what I needed to soothe my tattered nerves. When the pizza arrived, he placed slices on a couple of paper plates and then met me in the living room. He blessed the food and we began to eat.

I was trying to figure out a way to tell him about Sean, when he started talking. "I was thinking of a way to take your attention off things, at least for a little while, and then a great idea came to me."

"What did you have in mind?" I inquired between bites of pepperoni, green olives, and pineapple.

"Well, years ago, when I was married, my ex and I bought a timeshare in Aruba. When we divorced, I kept it as part of the settlement. I usually rent it out because it's such a romantic place to visit and I wasn't going to go alone. But if you're open to it, I'd love to take you. What do you think?" He held his breath while he waited for my response.

Aruba? Wow. I'd never been there before. Just the name alone sounded sexy. There was no way that I could tell him about Sean now. But maybe getting away would be just what I needed. Maybe, just maybe, it would give Cynthia time to cool off and I'd be gone when Sean returned to his old job. I was positive that Cynthia's hired gun wouldn't be able to follow me, although he'd really laid off me lately. The more I thought about it, the more I liked the idea. "When would we leave?"

"Well..." he said as he reached into his work bag on the floor. "I was thinking we could leave...tomorrow. I know I suggested going to church this Sunday, but we can go when we get back." And then he handed me two first-class plane tickets.

"Tomorrow? How in the world do you expect me to be ready by tomorrow?" My mind was racing. There was no way I could pull it together and be ready to board a plane by morning.

"Calm down. Calm down. All you need to do is pack your clothes and I'm taking care of everything else."

"What time would we leave?"

"Ten in the morning. We could be on the beach by five." His eyes begged me to say yes.

I took a deep breath and then slowly exhaled and nodded. "Okay. It sounds like fun. Thank you."

"Whoo hoo!" he said as he jumped up, taking me with him and spinning me around. "We are going to have a great time and you'll finally be able to relax." He set me down.

His excitement was infectious and I found myself getting as enthusiastic as he was. "I have to call Michele. She's going to be so thrilled for me. For us."

"You call her and I'll straighten up in here."

"Don't you need to go home and pack?"

"Nope," he said, shaking his head. "I knew you'd say yes, so my bags are packed and loaded in my truck."

I smiled at the man who was winning more of my heart with each day that passed. "Thank you," I said sincerely.

He stopped what he was doing so he could wrap his arms around me again. "When we get back, we'll figure out how to stop all this nonsense. I'm ready for us to get on with our lives, without all this drama in the background." He looked deep into my eyes and gave me a big kiss. "I'd do anything for you. I'd swim a swamp filled with crocodiles and alligators to get to you and make sure you're safe. You believe me, don't you?"

"Yes, I do," I said as I pulled his face back to mine and returned the kiss.

Chapter 27

"Hey, Chele!" I said, the joy in my voice tumbling out when she answered.

Michele chuckled. "Hey girl, what's got you so excited? You didn't sound anything like this when I was at your house."

"Rick! He's taking me on a two-week vacation to Aruba."

"You're kidding!"

"Nope, we leave in less than 12 hours."

"That's fabulous! How did that happen?"

"He wants me to get me away from all this madness."

"Oooh, I love him for you. Wait, how are you getting all this time off work?"

"That's a perk of being a partner," I laughed, then said, "but seriously, Mr. Jeffries knows I'm always available. I have a ton of vacation time I've never used and it carries over from year to year. Me being off for an extended amount of time is needed right now."

"Well, enjoy yourself. I'll check on your house while you're gone."

"Thanks. And don't tell Andrea. She'll use her key and there's no tellin' what I'll come home to!"

We laughed at my sister, both of us knowing her antics and what she was capable of. After chatting a few more moments, I hung up and started hunting for my suitcases in the basement.

"Hey, Sweetie," Rick yelled down. "You need any help?"

"I'm good. You've already done too much. I'll be ready before you know it."

After packing, we slept for a couple hours, then drove to the airport for our 6-hour flight, which was certain to be pure luxury. I was accustomed to flying coach, or maybe upgrading to business class, but first-class was a treat. Since we received priority boarding, the flight attendants served mimosas in actual glassware while the rest of the plane filled with passengers.

I looked out the window and watched the ground crew load our luggage, then turned to Rick. "Thank you again."

"I should be the one thanking you. I get to spend 14 days on a beautiful island with an even more beautiful woman, who I hope will be wearing little more than a bikini the entire time." I blushed, while he continued. "And who I hope will finally say the words I've been waiting to hear."

Knowing what he was talking about, I said anyway, "What words would those be?"

"Tonight is the night."

"We'll see…"

He raised his glass and clinked it with mine. "Here's to us."

We stared at each other as we sipped our drinks. Then I leaned my head back against the oversized comfy seat and took a long… slow… and deep cleansing breath.

As we taxied down the runway and the wheels folded into their hiding spots in the belly of the plane, I looked back out the window. I visualized myself leaving my problems on the ground while we climbed through the clouds and into the blue sky far above everything that plagued me.

"Good morning, may I take your order," a short and portly man in a red and blue uniform asked us, mentally bringing me back into my seat. He handed us a laminated card with 3 hot breakfast choices. We both selected scrambled eggs and toast and within moments we were enjoying a surprisingly good meal. I sipped a couple more mimosas and began reading a novel on my Kindle until my eyes tired and I used Rick's broad shoulder as my pillow. I felt him kiss the top of my head before I nodded off to sleep.

By the time we walked through customs at the tiny airport, my troubles were forgotten. Our cab driver zoomed us through the streets of Aruba while Rick gave me a little island history.

"Do you see the direction of the trees?" he asked as we made our way to our 5-star resort.

"Yes."

"You'll see that there's a constant breeze that causes the trees to grow in the direction of the wind. And because Aruba is basically a desert, they get very little rain. All the tropical foliage you see is imported."

I listened to him, and for the first time it was painfully obvious to me that he'd been here before. With another woman. His wife. I hoped that he wouldn't be thinking about her while he was here with me. "You know a lot about the island."

He covered my hand with his. "I know what's floating through your head, Chanelle. You're the only woman on my mind and in my heart."

"You mean it?"

He squeezed my hand and kissed me gently on the lips. "I mean it."

I grinned and settled in for the remainder of the ride to our new home for the next couple weeks. But walking into our suite was an experience I never anticipated.

"Rick! This place is huge." I went from room to room of the beachfront villa, taking in everything. The fully equipped kitchen with stainless steel appliances. The bathrooms, with his and hers sinks. The flat screen televisions in the two bedrooms and living room. But the best part of the suite was the wrap around balcony that stretched from the master bedroom to the living room. The bedroom view overlooked the sparkling water and the living room view overlooked the award winning golf course.

I stepped onto the balcony from the bedroom and leaned over the rail, looking out into the turquoise Caribbean Sea, filling my lungs with the fresh air. Rick tipped the porter then joined me.

"Isn't it beautiful," he said.

I nodded. "I've never seen water so clear."

"And it's only going to get better. Come on, let's hit up the pool," he said, as he clapped his hands together and then went back inside, opening up one of his suitcases and pulling out a pair of navy blue swimming trunks.

"Yes!" I followed him inside and opened up my 3 suitcases before finding my favorite orange and yellow bikini and matching sarong. I excused myself and went to the bathroom where I changed and wet my hair so that curly ringlets fell just below my shoulders. I put my sunglasses on top of my head to hold back my hair, applied sunblock to my face and sun tanning oil to my body. I slipped into a pair of thong wedges, filled my straw beach bag with all the essentials and moments later we were walking to the pool.

I'd been to some exclusive resorts in my life, but this one topped them all. The pool had an infinity edge and a swim up bar that included a popcorn machine and an ice cream dispenser. To the far right of the pool, there was a stone waterfall, which made the most tranquil sound as the falls descended from atop the mountain into the water below.

I claimed two lounging chairs underneath an umbrella that looked like a straw hut, while Rick grabbed a couple of towels from the towel stand. We spread them out on the chairs and then reclined. I closed my eyes as I lifted my face toward the heavens and allowed the Caribbean sun to heal my wounded and broken spirit. I surrendered all my cares to God as I said a silent prayer of thanks to Him for allowing me to experience this dream of an island. I was sure that I would have two weeks free of drama and fear.

"Would the lovely lady like a drink?" I opened my eyes to see the pool waiter standing over me.

"Mmmm... what do you recommend?"

"We have the Aruba Island Dream, which is a mix of flavored rums, mango, pineapple, and fresh squeezed orange juice," he said in an accent that sounded like he was born in Jamaica.

"Ooohhh, that sounds yummy. I'll have that."

"And for you, sir?" he asked, turning his attention to Rick.

"I'll have the same."

"Thank you. I'll be back in a moment."

As the waiter left, I gazed at Rick and paused before I asked him the question that had been in the back of my mind since we landed. "Are you sure you're okay being in the same space with me that you once shared with your ex?"

He hesitated briefly. "Well, I have to admit that it does feel a little weird. It's been so long since I've been to the island. When my ex and I first came here, we were so in love. By our last trip, our marriage was a shell of what it once was and I was hoping to recapture some of that passion. I wanted to remind her of what we once had in the hopes of having it again. Not only did it not work, but toward the end of our vacation she got a text from her boyfriend, while I had her phone." His eyes clouded over as he thought back. "Now that I'm here with you, I'm thinking of the possibilities of our future and I'm amped by it. I guess it'll just take me a moment to shift my thinking and keep it in the present and future; and not think about what happened here in my past. I know I'm rambling, but does that make sense?"

I shook off the guilt I was feeling because I wasn't being transparent with him, and took his hand in mine. "That makes perfect sense. And I appreciate you doing this for me."

Rick looked down at our hands and then into my eyes. "Chanelle, I'm really falling in love with you. I know you don't want to hear that, but it's true. I would do absolutely anything in the world for you."

"I know you would. Let's just enjoy the next two weeks and not think about your ex or my stalker." *Or my affair,* I added silently. "Once we get back, we'll work on a plan to bring this to an end. One way or another."

"Agreed."

Just then the waiter returned with our drinks.

"This is delicious," I said, as I savored my first sip.

"Thank you, ma'am. It's our resort specialty."

Rick signed for the bill and started our room tab. Then we sat by the pool and talked for hours, ordering drink after drink. At one point, we got in the water and swam up to the bar. We ordered ice cream and ate our cones while swirling our feet in the water, enjoying the private time we shared. Several times we had to reapply sunblock so we wouldn't burn in the island sun. My fingers tingled when I rubbed the lotion into his muscular back.

And my skin was on fire, and not from the sun, as he rubbed it on mine.

After we left the pool, we went back to the room and showered. Then changed into our evening clothes and went into town. Our pool attendant had recommended a sunset dinner at the Flying Fishbone, so he made the reservations for us, and the ambiance was almost indescribable. Most of the tables were on the beach or at the edge of the shore.

While we waited for our appetizers, we threw bread into the water and watched the small fish flock to the food and swim around our feet. As boats passed by, slight waves rolled in and gently washed up our legs.

Sitting across from Rick, staring into his eyes through the glow of the table candles, while the sun set, was the most sensual moment I'd ever experienced in my life. I thought about my ex and how this was something that we had never done in all the years we were together. And suddenly I felt cheated. I knew that I had given Michael too many years of my life, but until now, I had no comprehension of exactly what I had missed. Instead of being bitter, I quickly nixed the thought and returned my focus to Rick. It was at that very moment, that I felt myself tip over the edge of love. I was no longer fighting the feeling, but flowing with it instead. Rick was not a man who would hurt me and I was going to enjoy being in love with him. It didn't matter that all of this had happened with lightning speed. When it's real, it's real. And this was definitely real.

"A penny for your thoughts." His voice interrupted my internal dialogue.

I gave him a coy smile. "Just that this is the happiest and most peaceful moment of my life. And I'm so glad to be here with you."

He smiled back. "I feel the same way, Chanelle." He reached across the table and grabbed my hands. "Sooo... do you think tonight will be the night when we can physically express how much we care about each other?"

I hated to dash the hope I saw in his eyes, but I knew that I still wasn't ready to take that step, especially as I held my secret. "How about we don't plan it, but just let it happen naturally?"

"Is that your way of saying no?"

I laughed a little. "That's my way of saying when it's the right time, you won't have to ask."

He exhaled deeply. "Okay. I can live with that."

Just then, the waitress arrived with our order. Our conversation took on a lighter tone as we chatted about the things we wanted to do while on the island. We agreed to do some things that he had never done before so we could start to build our own memories.

The next two weeks went by in a blur. Every day was filled with lots of fun in the sun. We spent time at the beach and in the pool. We parasailed, jet ski'd, rode ATV's, toured the island, swam in the natural pool, snorkeled, and went scuba diving. Every evening we had intimate dinners either on a sunset sail dinner cruise, at one of the several restaurants on the island, or on the beach. We did lots of shopping and shipped our purchases to Michele's home so we wouldn't have to take them back on the plane. The island had several casinos and some afternoons we would enjoy the air conditioning and free drinks while playing the slots. I was saddened when I realized that we only had one more night on the island.

"Hey, is everything okay?" Rick asked me as we sat on the couch in the villa watching an old episode of NCIS Los Angeles.

"Yeah, I just thought about how tonight is our last night and I got a little sad, that's all."

"I can't believe it's been two weeks already," Rick said sharing similar feelings. «The time sure did fly by."

"Yes it did." I just knew that I would have found the right time to tell Rick about Sean. But the closest I came was when we were strolling along the beach, my hand in his, my head resting on his shoulder. We'd stopped to watch the sunset and just held each other. I'd looked up at him and opened my mouth to confess, but he'd bent down and kissed me.

And that's what kept happening. Every time I got ready to open up and be honest, he would do something or say something sweet to me and I couldn't risk telling him and then losing him. Now we were just hours away from boarding a plane to head home and he was no closer to knowing my secret than he was when we first arrived.

I knew that I had to tell him before we left. Even if he was mad at me, he would have to sit next to me on the plane and I could try and convince him that I was still a good person with a good heart who made a mistake. I decided I finally had enough courage to come clean about my past and the reason for the stalking. I grabbed the remote and muted the television. Then I turned to face Rick.

I prayed that he would understand, took a deep breath, and then said, "I have something I need to tell you."

The concern I saw in Rick's eyes broke my heart. Would he have the same level of concern once he heard what I had to say? "Chanelle, what's wrong? Throughout this entire vacation, you've had these moments where you looked like you wanted to say something and then you don't."

He was so perceptive. "That's because you're right. I have wanted to tell you something for several weeks, but I've been afraid of your response."

"Whatever it is, it won't change how I feel about you. I told you that I love you. As a matter of fact, I have something for you. Wait right here." Rick jumped up before I had a chance to protest and went into the bedroom. He returned moments later with a small box and sat next to me.

He opened the box and revealed a gorgeous ruby ring in a platinum setting. "I have loved you since college. The day you walked into Lowe's and back into my life was the best day of my life. I hope you know by now that I am not the same man you left all those years ago. I want to love you. Cherish you. Provide for you. Protect you. I know you aren't ready to say yes to marriage, but will you say yes to being my woman? With a promise of more to come. Let me love you, Chanelle."

I stared at him, in complete shock. I pushed all my former apprehension aside and was more than ready to be in a committed relationship with Rick. "Yes, I accept your promise to love me. To cherish me. Provide for me. And protect me." I smiled and held out my right hand. He slid the ring on my finger and gave me a soft kiss.

"Oh, what was it that my beautiful lady wanted to tell me?" he asked me, as he stared lovingly into my eyes.

"Uh, it wasn't important." I gave him a feeble smile. I knew that I would have to tell him about Sean, but clearly today was not the day. I only hoped that he would still keep his promise to me once he found out the truth.

"You sure?"

I pulled his face within inches of mine. "Yes, I'm sure. But there is something that is important."

"And what's that?"

"Tonight is the night."

His eyes lit up. "You wouldn't play with a brother's heart would you?"

"I'd never play with your heart." I stood, pulling him with me. "You asked me to let you love me. Now I'm asking you to let me do the same." I beckoned for him to follow me and I could feel his eyes watching my behind as though I didn't have on a sundress.

I led him to the edge of my bed and motioned for him to sit. "Don't move," I commanded.

I could practically see his chest thumping through his shirt as he anticipated what was to come. I set my iPod to my "Slow and Sexy" playlist and did a striptease that would have made Holly Madison proud. We explored each other's bodies while we consummated our newly confessed love. But the best part of our night, was being nuzzled his arms as I floated off to sleep.

Chapter 28

"Tell me everything and don't leave anything out," Michele said as she reached our table at our favorite bar and grill at the mall. Michele wanted to hear all about our vacation, so she and I agreed to meet for lunch and do some girl bonding the Saturday after I returned. I was still slightly skittish about being out in public, not knowing if I was being watched, but I had to push past living my life in perpetual fear.

"It was amazing," I said as I motioned for our waiter. After placing our orders, we resumed our conversation. "You know all of my mistakes. My failed relationships. My bad choices. I don't deserve a man like Rick, but he's the best thing that's ever happened to me."

"He is a great man for you, Chanelle."

I nodded. "I know. I feel so unworthy of the devotion and intimacy and adoration he's pouring on me. And those two weeks together strengthened our connection."

"Soooo, did you finally give in?" she asked.

I blushed. "How could I not? And it was by far the most incredible time I've ever had with a man. Even in all my years with Michael, I never experienced anything as special as what happened with Rick. And he gave me this," I said, holding out my hand so she could get a good look at my new ring.

She brought my hand up to her face. "This is gorgeous!"

"I know, right? It's what made me give in." I giggled.

"Whew," she said, releasing my hand and leaning back in her seat. "That man loves you. Don't mess it up."

"I'm not."

"Did you tell him about Sean and Cynthia?"

"Uh, I didn't get a chance to."

"So then you *are* messing it up."

"No, I'm not. I looked for the right moment to say something, but it never came. Maybe that was a sign from God to keep my mouth shut," I said, twirling my new ring around my finger.

"Seriously? You're putting you being a coward on God?"

I frowned at my best friend. "I'm not being a coward. Look, we were Cynthia and Sean free for 14 whole days. I'm going to wait and see if, while we were gone, Sean talked some sense into Cynthia. I don't see a reason to spill my guts and risk my relationship if I no longer have a problem."

"I want to be sure I'm understanding your foolishness. Your barometer for determining whether or not you still have a problem is when you hear from Sean, Cynthia, or a STALKER again? What if by then, it's too late?"

"I hear you, but let's be done with this conversation. There's too much at stake for me to say something right now."

"Chanelle, there's too much at stake for you to not say something."

But I vehemently shook my head. "Unh uh. I've waited too long to find someone special. I hate to think that a decision I made months ago, darn near a year ago, could come back to haunt me and ruin my future."

Michele, forever the optimist, said, "I think you'll be pleasantly surprised by his response. Just trust him."

"Nope. Now, do you want to see my pictures from our trip?" I asked, deliberating turning the conversation to something more upbeat.

Michele sighed deeply and I saw disappointment etched in her wrinkled eyebrows. She couldn't understand the position I was in because she already had the dream life. I was still trying to create mine. "Yeah, show me your pics."

"I'm going to pretend you're eager to see them," I said, whipping out my iPad.

"I do want to see them. I'm just worried about you. That's all."

"I know. But let's enjoy our day together and not think about the dark side of my life right now. Deal?"

She hesitated before saying, "Deal."

Our waiter arrived with our meals and we began eating. Through bites of my jalepeno cheddar burger, I proceeded to tell Michele about our activities while in Aruba as I narrated the slideshow. Eventually, she lightened up and began enjoying her afternoon with me.

"Ben and I are definitely adding Aruba to our Bucket List!" Michele declared after viewing the last picture.

"You're gonna love it!"

We continued chatting about lighter subjects, though in the back of my mind, I couldn't shake her words: *What if by then, it's too late...*

Chapter 29

"Let the church say 'amen'," Pastor Sharpe said from the pulpit.

"Amen!"

"You may be seated."

Rick and I sat next to each other and I was beaming. In all the years Michael and I had been together, he never once set foot inside of a church.

"Church, this morning's message is: How Honest Are You? How…Honest…Are…You?"

Michele, who was sitting to my left, looked over at me and I could feel her eyes boring into the side of my face, though I continued looking straight ahead.

Pastor Sharpe continued. "In today's society, people find all kinds of reasons to justify being dishonest. Some say, 'oh, it's just a little white lie'. But what did they just tell?"

"A lie!" someone shouted.

"Or someone tells a lie by omission. What is that, church? They know the truth about something, but they allow you to think something different. They don't set the record straight. Well, I'm setting the record straight right now. A lie, is a lie, is a lie."

"Amen!" That darn Amen corner shouted their vocal agreement, as though they were perfect and never guilty of a little dishonesty.

"But what does God say? Proverbs 12:22 says: lying lips are an abomination to the Lord, but those who act faithfully are His delight. Are your lips lying, Church?"

"No," the lying Amen corner said.

"How can we change these lying lips? Simple. Tell the truth!"

"Preach!"

Pastor Sharpe continued to talk about the virtues of being honest and how no good comes from lying.

Rick leaned in, grabbed my hand, and said, "I like your pastor. She's on point. Without honesty, you have nothing."

I nodded my agreement and felt a churning in my stomach. "Do you have anything you want to tell me?" he asked.

I bit my bottom lip and shook my head, unable to speak.

"Good," he continued. "Because I have nothing I'm holding back from you either." He squeezed my hand, kissed my cheek, and turned his attention back to the sermon.

I took a deep slow breath and vowed to tell him the truth, the whole truth, and nothing but the truth. Please help me God!

Chapter 30

"Boss Lady! You're back!" Patty exclaimed the following Monday. She came from around her desk and pulled me into her plump bosom. "You shoulda told me you was comin' back. I woulda had your office decorated."

I chuckled and returned the hug. "You're too kind, but I just decided last night that enough was enough."

She lowered her voice. "Have you heard anything more from that stalker?"

I glanced around, even though I knew we were the only two in my suite. "Not a peep in well over three weeks. I'm thinking I'm in the clear."

"Oh, good, Boss Lady. I'm so happy this nightmare is over for you."

"You and me both."

"Did you ever find out who was behind it?"

"Uh, not really."

"Well, I'm just glad it's done. You go get settled and I'll buzz Mr. Jeffries and let him know you're back."

"Thank you, Patty," I said, turning and walking into my office. About five minutes later, I heard a familiar voice.

"Chanelle!" Mr. Jeffries said, entering my office and swiftly crossing the floor to hug me.

"Hello, Mr. Jeffries," I said returning his hug.

The older gentleman didn't waste any time. "I have a surprise for you." He turned to the door and said, "Come on in."

"Hey, Chanelle," Sean said from the doorway.

"Uh, hey, Sean."

"Isn't it wonderful?" Mr. Jeffries offered. "I was ecstatic when Sean called and told me he was retuning to Michigan."

"Yes," I managed to choke out, "it is wonderful. Welcome back, Sean."

"Well, I'll leave you two to get caught up." Mr. Jeffries gave me a second hug and exited my office.

"Chanelle, it's so good to see you after all these months."

I stared at him, examining my feelings, and praying that I wouldn't feel anything. And I was completely relieved when I did a gut check and there was…nothing. Nothing about me was still interested in Sean. I'd found the man I loved… and who was free to love me back.

And that man was now walking through my door. Carrying a bouquet of roses. Yellow and white roses. The same kind of roses Sean had sent me, giving me the worst case of déjà vu I'd ever experienced.

If it was possible, I would have crawled under my desk and hid until both of them left.

"Hey, Sweetie," he said, walking past Sean as though he weren't in the room, handing me my flowers, and planting a big kiss on my lips.

"Uh, hey, Babe. What brings you by?" I stammered.

"It's your first day back and I'm proud of you."

Sean lost the smile he was just wearing and coughed, announcing his presence in my office. "Oh, uh, Babe, I'd like you to meet one of my co-workers." *And my ex-lover who I'm praying doesn't say anything.* "Sean, this is my…boyfriend, Rick."

"Nice to meet you," Rick said, extending his hand.

Sean reluctantly shook it and tried hard to compose himself. I held my breath and prayed. "Nice to meet you also. You have a very special woman," he said, staring at me a little harder than he should, causing me even more discomfort.

Rick placed a possessive arm around my waist and forcefully pulled me to him. "Tell me something I don't know," he said, bending down to kiss me again. If he'd lifted his leg like a dog, he'd have been less obvious in marking his territory.

"Sweetheart, I have to get to work," he said. "But let's go out to dinner tonight and celebrate your first day back."

"I'd like that. You pick the place."

"Okay, Babe." He kissed me a third time, and then said, "It was nice meeting you, Shane."

"Nice to meet you also. And it's Sean."

"My bad. Sean."

He winked at me and left my office.

"So, how long has that been going on?" Sean demanded, as though he had a right.

"It's none of your business," I hissed. "I told you that I wasn't waiting for you to figure out what you wanted to do. Not to mention, your *wife* hired someone to *threaten* me in order to get me to back away from you. Why would you think I'd stick around for that?"

He walked up on me and said, "I tell you that I'm leaving my wife for you. Walking away from my marriage for us to have a chance together. And this is what you do to me?" His low tone shook me just a tad.

I'd never seen this side of Sean. I swallowed my rising fear. "That was your choice. I never asked you to leave your wife. And you need to back away from me. Now."

"I came back to Michigan for you. This isn't over. We aren't over." Slowly, he leaned in and kissed me on my cheek, then walked out of my office. Leaving me dazed.

Chapter 31

"Tell me about your coworker?" Rick said over our candlelight celebratory dinner.

Although, with the way my first day back had gone, I didn't see anything worth celebrating. "There's nothing to tell. He's just someone I work with."

Rick took a bite of his T-bone steak and chewed methodically before speaking. "Chanelle, do you remember the night I came to your house after we saw each other in Lowe's?" When I nodded, he continued. "And I told you about how my marriage fell apart?" I nodded again. "My marriage ended because my wife cheated on me. She was a liar." I squirmed in my seat. "And I could see through her lies."

"I remember."

"And remember when we were sitting on your couch and I told you that I can tell when you're being dishonest?"

I gulped. "Yes."

"And remember how your pastor just preached on honesty?"

"Yes, but what point are you making?"

"Something is up with you. Our relationship will never work if we're not honest with each other. If you have anything you need to tell me, now's the time."

I absently twirled my promise ring and carefully considered my next words. I felt like Michele was on one of my shoulders telling me to be honest and he'd understand. And on my other shoulder was Andrea, telling me I was a punk if I said anything. "I... uh... there's nothing to tell."

He stared at me with laser focus. "Nothing?"

I shook my head, committing myself to my deception. "Nope. Nothing to tell."

"And the guy in your office? The one who was looking at you like you belonged to him and looking at me like I was in the way? There's nothing to tell me about that?"

I sipped my water and tried to hide myself behind the goblet. Then I slowly shook my head again and ignored the warning bells in my head. "Like I said, there's nothing to tell. He's just a colleague."

"For the sake of our future, I hope you're being straight with me, Chanelle."

"I am." I reached across the table to hold his hands. "Now can we go back to enjoying a beautiful dinner?"

"Yeah," he said, still giving me look that let me know he wasn't buying what I was unconvincingly selling.

Chapter 32

"Good morning, Chanelle," Sean said, standing in my doorway.

It was Thursday and I'd successfully avoided him for a couple days, but Mr. Jeffries had given me another huge prospect and the only way for me to land the account was to work with Sean. After all, that was the reason he'd been rehired, and I was Mr. Jeffries "go to" person when it came to the larger accounts. "Good morning, Sean. Please come in and have a seat at the table," I said, standing and coming from behind my desk.

I didn't want him in my office. I didn't want him anywhere near me. But working with him wasn't optional. I only hoped and prayed he'd be able to stay focused on the task in front of us and leave behind all thoughts of rekindling an intimate relationship.

"Please leave it open," I instructed as he started to close my door.

"I thought you'd want it closed so we wouldn't be interrupted."

I bet you did. "Patty will make sure we're not disturbed." I met him at the table and said, "Have you given any thought to how we can start outlining this account? This is a very important client for Mr. Jeffries."

"You sound so formal. I was hoping we could spend some time catching up."

I gave a very loud sigh. "Sean, I don't have time to chat. We have to get the ball rolling on this project."

"So, you're just going to pretend that we didn't have anything? That there was no chemistry between us?"

I threw my hands in the air. "I'm not pretending anything. Yes, we had amazing chemistry. But it's over now. Why can't you understand and respect that? Not to mention, again, that your *wife* threatened me. Where is she anyway? Were you able to finally talk to her? Because I haven't heard from her in a few weeks." I hoped by switching topics to Cynthia, I could take his focus off us. Besides, I needed to know if I should still be worried.

"Cynthia moved back into our house in Virginia when I relocated here. I honestly don't know what's going on with her these days, but she's actually being served with divorce papers today."

"Wow, so you're going through with it?"

"I told you, I want a chance with you."

"Sean," I began, praying that I could get through to him, "that's no longer possible. But back to Cynthia. How do you think she's going to take the news?"

"No clue," he said, as his cell rang. He checked the number and said, "I guess I'm about to find out." He swiped the screen to the right and before he could say one word, I heard Cynthia yelling.

"Are you freakin' kiddin' me? You divorcing me? For that tramp?"

"Please calm down," Sean said. "She's not a tramp and our divorce has nothing to do with her. We've talked about this."

"If it wasn't for her, you'd be hear wit me, right now. I was willin' to forgive you and start over. But I see how it is. So both of you better watch yo back. You tell that slutty home wrecker that I ain't through wit her."

"Cyn—." That was as far as he got, because she hung up on him.

Though the sun was shining brightly through my windows, inside my office was as gray as the skies before a tornado. I knew that the nightmare that I prayed and prayed and prayed was over, was about to be kicked up a notch. And there was no way we were all coming out of this alive.

"Michele, I never thought I'd say this, but Sean is as loco as his wife," I said.

"So, Cynthia is after you because you slept with her husband and he's divorcing her? And Sean is after you because you've moved on with your life and don't want him? This is ridiculous."

"You think?" I said, sarcastically. "This kind of stuff only happens to me. But I'm thinking maybe I should call Steve."

"For once, you are saying something that makes sense. Are you finally going to tell Rick?"

"You're kidding, right? I told you how Rick was acting when he came to my office. And then when we had dinner and he asked me point-blank if there was anything to tell about Sean and I couldn't bring myself to do it. Now I can't tell him."

"You've really dug a hole for yourself," she said, taking a bite of a tortilla chip with guacamole.

I looked at my best friend and exhaled loudly. "I know. I know. And there is no way out of it without somebody getting hurt. Physically and/or emotionally. That's why I need to talk to Steve."

Michele pulled out her phone. "I'll see if he can swing by when he gets off work. How long do you plan on hanging out with me?"

I'd come by her house when I'd gotten off work and had already been here for a few hours. "Not much longer. I told Rick I'd be home by 9:00."

"Sounds like you two are living together."

"I guess we kinda are."

"Do you still have him sleeping on the couch?"

"He's been upgraded to the guest bedroom," I said, smiling.

"But not your bed?

I shook my head. "Not yet."

"So no more since Aruba? How are you holding out? And why are you holding out?"

"My conscience. Too much going on for me to keep adding layers of emotions. Anyway, call Steve. I'd like to see if he can come by while I'm here. Otherwise, maybe we can meet up tomorrow."

Michele dialed her brother, and after finding out that he was working the second half of a double shift, he agreed to meet me at my office the next day. With the one condition that he was dressed in plain clothes.

"Are you going to tell Steve everything?"

"I'm not sure yet. Probably. Maybe. I don't know…"

"Steve's a cop. He's heard and seen it all. Just be straightforward with him."

"Yeah, yeah. But he hasn't heard it from me."

"He loves you like family, so keep it real with him."

"We'll see. Look, I'm going to get out of here. I'll let you know how things go tomorrow." I stood and gave my bestie a hug, then went home.

Fortunately, Rick didn't bring up any prickly topics and I had a peaceful night. But the next morning, as I was sitting across from Steve in my office, I was feeling anything but peaceful.

"What's been going on, Chanelle? And be straight up with me."

"Promise not to judge me?"

"Have I ever?"

"You got me there. Okay. Here's my life for the last nine or so months." I told Steve everything. The affair. The bad dates. Reconnecting with Rick. The Stalker who seemed to have vanished. Cynthia calling and being outside my home. The shooting lessons. My lies to Rick. Sean returning to Michigan and his possessive behavior. And I concluded with Cynthia's threat to me via her conversation with her husband yesterday. "So I'm telling you all this because I'm on edge right now. And I don't want to ruin my new relationship." I looked at the floor, unable to face Steve. I knew it was bad, but saying everything out loud made me feel like a horrible person.

"Is this an on or off the record conversation we're having?"

"Well, I'd love for it to be an off the record brother/sister discussion."

He studied me. "So you want Steve, your brother, to fix this and not Steven, the cop?"

"Yes."

He leaned back in the chair, with his hands in his lap, circling his thumbs around each other. "What has you the most concerned?"

"Honestly?"

"Honestly."

"Sean. Because I have to work with him almost every day and he's not hearing me when I tell him we're completely over."

"Hmmm. I thought you would have said Cynthia."

I shook my head. "She's in Virginia. Sean is here. In my face."

He bobbed his head slowly. "I'll handle him."

"What are you gonna do?"

"Don't worry about it. You need plausible deniability. Just leave it to me. He's done being a problem for you."

I leaned forward in my seat. "You're not going to hurt him, are you?"

And his eyes squinted. "Would you care?"

Slowly, I fell back into my chair, creating distance between myself and my almost brother. "I, uh, I…I wouldn't care, *care*, but, I mean, I wouldn't want him to get hurt."

"Look, lil sis," he began, smirking at me, "don't sweat it. Just go about your business and let me do what I do."

I nodded and stood with him. After giving him a hug and escorting him out of my office, I rushed back to my couch, plopped down, and called Michele."

"Has Steven gone crazy?"

"What are you talking about?"

"I think he might beat up Sean," I whispered into my cell phone.

"What? That's not Steve."

"I didn't think so. But I told him everything and he told me he would 'handle Sean'. I think he's gonna beat him up."

"He would never put his career on the line like that. I'm sure that's not it."

"Maybe," I said, clearly skeptical. "But that's how I took it."

"Well, just act natural and let whatever's gonna happen, play out."

"O…K…, I'll talk to you later."

After hanging up, I chewed on my fingernail, thinking about what I may have just done. Did I set Sean up to get hurt without realizing it? I thought about how Steve was when we were growing up. He was the same age as Andrea and had been on the gangsta side of the law, until he got in trouble in high school and did a 180 degree turn. His story was similar to Judge Mathis, only he didn't become a judge, he became a cop. And he'd always been an honorable officer, with awards to back it up. I hoped that my mess wasn't going to have him flip back to the shady side of life.

But six hours later, my fears became an awful reality. "Chanelle," Mr. Jeffries said, entering my office and closing the door before I had a chance to blink.

"Mr. Jeffries, is everything okay?"

"No, it's not. Sean's been arrested. I just heard from his boss at Image."

"He's been what?"

"Arrested."

My eyes widened. "Oh my gosh, for what?"

"Embezzlement from his employer in Virginia."

"Excuse me? I can't imagine Sean being arrested for anything, let alone embezzlement."

"Well he was. He was picked up about an hour ago."

I shook my head, confused. "Picked up from where?"

"Image."

"I, I don't understand."

"Apparently, there was a complaint filed against him and a bench warrant for his arrest. He was pulled over for a traffic violation on his way back from lunch and when they ran his license, the warrant popped up."

This had to be the work of Steve. But how did he create a false charge and get a warrant for Sean's arrest so quickly?

"That's awful news, Mr. Jeffries. Is Image going to stand by him?"

"No idea. But that's not something we can tolerate. I'll be pulling him from all future projects until he's able to clear his name. And if he can't, then he will no longer be a consultant for our firm."

I felt a mixture of relief and disloyalty. I'd betrayed a former friend, but at least now I wouldn't have to see him everyday. I wasn't sure if this was a win for me or not.

Mr. Jeffries misread the look on my face and said, "Don't worry, Chanelle. I know how close the two of you were. But we'll get someone else to partner with you. Sean was excellent, but no one is irreplaceable. Not even you or me."

The elderly gentleman laughed, but I didn't. Enfolded in what he'd just said was a warning to me. If he ever found out about my indiscretions, he'd terminate my partnership first and ask questions later.

I gave him a smile that probably looked more like a grimace. "Well, keep me posted."

Mr. Jeffries nodded and walked out of my office. I picked up my cell phone to call Steve, and saw a text from him. It read: *Everyone has skeletons.*

I was no longer comfortable talking about this at work, so I grabbed my purse and walked out into the open area of my suite. Patty wasn't at her desk, so I left her a quick note that I was taking off a little early and to call me on my mobile if she needed to reach me. Then I raced to my car and called Steve.

"What did you do?" I asked the second he answered.

"I told you I'd handle it. Wanna meet?"

"Yes, the park around the corner from my house?"

"See you there in 15."

I didn't even bother to say goodbye before I hung up. I bowed my head while sitting behind my steering wheel and said a quick prayer to God. Then sped to the park to wait.

Chapter 33

"Steve, what did you do?" I asked in a panic, before he even had a chance to sit down.

He was now wearing his uniform and looked like the cop I thought he was. "Settle down. I didn't do anything. His background did it for me."

I knitted my brows together. "What are you talking about?"

"Here," he said, handing me an envelope. "Take a look at this."

"What is it?"

"Read it and see," he said, taking a seat next to me on the park bench.

I opened the envelope and was astonished to see a rap sheet. Sean's rap sheet. I read through the laundry list of charges and darn near had to pick up my mouth, which was close to touching the ground. I looked at Steve in amazement. "Sean did all of this?"

"Allegedly he did. The warrant for his arrest was real."

I closed my eyes and put my head in my hands. "This is insane. There's no way that Sean embezzled money from Handle Marketing."

"That's something he's going to have to prove and he'll get his day in court. He's being extradited back to Virginia. Authorities there have already been notified and the paperwork is in process for them to come get him."

"I won't believe it. That's not his character."

"Look, I can't answer that. All I know is you had a problem and I told you I'd take care of it. And it's been taken care of. Let me know if you hear from Cynthia and we'll deal with her. But at this point, if Sean was the only one you were worried about, then you should be in the clear."

"Steve, I don't know how to thank you. I hope you didn't do anything that would put your job in jeopardy."

"I'm not the guy I was years back. I'm all about law and order. But if you dig deep enough into people's past, you'll always be able to uncover something you can use. And your boy proved that to be true." He stood and tussled my hair, the way he does Michele. "I gotta get back to work. You know how to find me if you need me." He kissed the top of my head and walked out of the park, leaving me sitting on the bench and wondering what to do next.

Chapter 34

"That was delicious," Rick said, licking the last of the barbecue sauce from his fingers.

"I'm glad you enjoyed it." I smiled, taking our plates into the kitchen and loading them into the dishwasher.

Rick followed me. "Let me help you clean up."

I swatted him. "Absolutely not. You've done so much for me lately. Let me enjoy doing this for you. Why don't you go into the den and watch a little TV. I'll join you as soon as I'm finished in here."

"You sure you don't want some help?"

"I'm positive. Now go." I shooed him away.

I quickly straightened the kitchen, then curled up next to him on the couch. "What are you watching?"

"Nothing really, just flipping through the channels. Do you have anything you'd like to watch?"

"Well, you know how I love me some ratchet reality TV." I laughed.

"Absolutely not. I value my brain cells and I will not waste them on that garbage."

He was so adamant that I didn't tell him that I watched all of the shows. The Housewives, Basketball Wives, Love and Hip Hop. All of them. "How about a movie?" I offered.

"Now you're talking my language."

I slid off the couch. "Okay, you pick the movie and I'll pop some popcorn."

"K. Comedy or Drama?"

"Hmmm… Let's do a comedy. I could use a good laugh." I hummed on my way to the kitchen. For the first time in months, I felt normalcy in my life. Just as Steve had told me, Sean was taken back to Virginia. In my heart, I didn't believe he was guilty of what he was being accused of doing. But being Sean and Cynthia free for the past week eased my guilt substantially. I'd managed to keep my secret from Rick and his trust in me seemed to be growing. We'd had a great couple's weekend with Ben and Michele and we were enjoying a Sunday evening before we started our workweek. Yes, my life had made the U-turn I was praying for and was thankfully headed in the right direction.

I whistled as I grabbed the jar of popcorn kernels from the cabinet, poured some into the air popper and turned it on. I glanced at my cell phone laying on the counter and saw that I'd missed a call. I dialed my voicemail before grabbing a bowl to catch the popcorn. I froze in my tracks when I heard the voice.

"Hey, Chanelle. It's me. Sean. I only have a minute to talk. Literally, that's all they give you in jail. But I wanted you to know that I didn't do what I'm being accused of and my name will be cleared soon. Though, I'm pretty sure Mr. Jeffries won't be taking me back. But, um, I also think you should know that Cynthia is blaming you for my arrest. I tried talking sense into her, but she's not listening. Being locked up, there's nothing I can do to help you, so I thought I'd warn you. I tried telling the cell block guard in my ward, but to him, I'm just a con, so he's not listening. Cynthia is hell-bent on making you pay. I—I—I'm sorry, Chanelle. I never meant for this to happen to you. I love you. And I wanted us to be together. I still want us to be together. But I think you should watch your back. I'll try and call you later. Bye, Love."

Moments later, Rick came into the kitchen. "Babe, what's taking you so long? The movie…" Rick's voice trailed off when he saw me standing in the middle of the kitchen surrounded by popcorn. "What happened?"

He noticed the cell phone still in my hand and took it from me. "Did The Stalker call you?"

I was trying desperately to snap out of my catatonic state. I had to think fast. "Um, no. No, he didn't. I, um, I…" Think, Chanelle, think. I willed myself to come up with a believable story.

"Well, if it wasn't him, then what has you so frightened?"

I took my phone back and set it on the counter. "Uh… I… uh… um, I just got a voicemail from work. Uh, Patty just, um, Patty said she won't be in tomorrow because her husband got hurt at work today and he's in the hospital."

"Oh, no! That's terrible. Is he going to be okay?"

I settled into my lie. "Oh, yes," I said quickly. "He's—he's going to be fine. He should be able to come home in a day or so."

"That's good news." Rick embraced me. "You had me scared. You looked like you'd seen a ghost or something."

I couldn't look at him, so I turned my head slightly and looked down. "Sorry to scare you. But all is well." I removed his arms from around my waist and headed to the closet to grab the broom and dustpan. "Why don't you go back into the den and restart the movie. I'll clean up this mess and be there in a sec."

"Okay. Don't take too long." He kissed my cheek and walked out of the room. But not before stealing a quick glance at my cell phone.

I breathed a huge sigh of relief that was short lived. Rick swallowed my lie this time, but it didn't go down easy and he was a very smart man. I knew next time I wouldn't be so lucky.

Chapter 35

I turned on the water in the sink in the downstairs bathroom. "Hey, girl," I said in a hushed tone.

"Hey, Chanelle! Why are you whispering?" Michele asked.

"Because I don't want Rick to hear me. I just got a voicemail from Sean and I lied about it."

"This makes absolutely no sense. Why aren't you honest with the man? A relationship built on lies isn't a relationship."

"Look, I didn't call you for a lecture," I said with way more attitude than I should have had. "I called because I need your help."

"You've got a lot of nerve. You don't want to hear my opinion, but you want my help."

"Exactly. So can you meet me tomorrow for lunch?" I ignored the irritation in Michele's voice because she had every right to be agitated with me.

There was a moment of silence. "Fine," she relented. "When and where?"

"Ruby Tuesday's, tomorrow at noon."

"I'll be there."

"Thanks. Talk to you later." I disconnected the call.

"Over here." I stood slightly and waved to Michele to join me in a booth in the back of the restaurant.

Michele snaked her way through the tables. "What in the world do you have on?" she asked, sitting across from me and placing her purse beside her.

"What do you mean?"

"I mean, you look like you're dressed to drive a 1960's convertible with those oversized dark glasses and that scarf." Michele was trying hard to contain her laughter.

"Shhhhh… lower your voice. I don't want anyone to recognize me."

"It's official. You have finally lost your mind."

"Whatever." I pulled my cell phone and a piece of paper out of my bag. "Here, listen to this." I pressed play on Sean's voicemail message and handed the phone to Michele.

Her mouth dropped when she heard the message. When it was over, she gave me back my phone. "Oh, my God," she said, leaning back in her seat. She had to pause what she was going to say because the waitress arrived at our table. We placed our orders and then, Michele continued. "Did you call Steve?"

I removed my sunglasses and set them on the table. "Unh uh. He helped me enough with Sean. I thought about this a lot last night, and I have an idea."

"I'm listening…" Though her facial expression told a different story.

"I think we should go after Cynthia."

Michele threw her hands up in exasperation. "Why would we do that? It seems very dangerous."

"I disagree. Don't football players say the best defense is a great offense?"

"I have no idea if they say that or not. But it doesn't matter because you're not a football player. And this isn't a game." Michele paused while the waitress brought our drinks and salads. "Let me make sure I have this straight. You don't want to do the logical thing and call the police. Or even call Steve again. Instead, you'd rather confront Cynthia?"

"Well, when you say it like that, you make me sound ridiculous."

"That's because you are ridiculous! Chanelle, this is not a good idea."

"But think about it," I pleaded with her. "No one would see it coming." I took a sip of my iced tea and leaned back in the booth as though I'd said something profound. "I think my idea is absolutely brilliant."

Michele just stared at me. After a few moments she said, "I'm at a total loss for words."

I ignored her. "Plus, I've been holding on to some information that I think may be useful." I grabbed the piece of paper that I'd removed from my bag and slid it in front of Michele.

She looked down at it. "What's this?"

"That is the license plate number from Cynthia's car. I wrote it down the day she was in front of my house before I went on vacation," I said triumphantly.

"O...K... And what do you propose we do with this?" Michele was clearly confused.

"We use it to track her down. Duh..."

"Uh, why can't you just ask Sean where she is?"

"Because he's locked up. He doesn't know where she is. And it's not like he's at a country club and can make calls whenever he feels like it. If he calls me again and I can get the information, then fine. Otherwise, let's use this," I said, pointing to the piece of paper, "and track her down."

She stared at me. "You're really serious about this."

"I'm absolutely serious. I'm guessing that it's a rental. And even though she's been leaving me alone, she must be coming back to town or she's going to put that stalker on me again. Otherwise, why would Sean warn me to watch my back?"

I knew it would take some coaxing to get Michele onboard with my plan, so I played my ace in the hole. "Michele, I need you. I need this nightmare to end and I can't do it alone. You're my sister from another mister. Please help me. Please."

"And there's no way I can convince you to call Steve?"

"Like I said, he just helped me out. And I think we have enough to do this ourselves. But if we can't find the information on our own or it gets too dangerous, then we can call Steve."

I could see her thinking about it and I held my breath and prayed that she would say yes. "I'll help you on one condition."

I exhaled. "Anything! You name it."

"I'll help you if you come clean with Rick. About everything." Now it was her turn to sip her lemonade and lean back in the booth.

Ugh! I knew she would pull a stunt like this. Fortunately, the waitress arrived with our entrees, which bought me time to plan how I was going to respond.

"Okay. But I get to decide when."

"That works. As long as it's within the next week."

"How about the next two weeks?"

"Agreed." She held out her hand for me to shake.

"Agreed," I said, as I shook her hand. "Now let me tell you my plan."

We leaned in toward each other and I told her how we were going to bring Cynthia down and I was going to get my life back.

Chapter 36

"Do you really have to leave?" I asked. It was Sunday evening, and we were sitting on my couch in the den. Rick had just told me that he was staying at his house tonight and leaving early in the morning to drive to Chicago for a contractor's convention.

"I'm so sorry, Chanelle. But I have to go."

"And you're leaving tomorrow? Why didn't you tell me about it sooner?"

"Because I just decided today that it's important for me to go. I've gone for years and it's always led to a lot of business. I was going to cancel my reservation because of what was going on with you, but since we haven't heard from him in weeks, I figured you'd be safe. Besides, I'll only be gone for four days. Please try to understand."

"I'm trying, but what if they pop back up while you're gone?" I whined.

Rick frowned. "They? I thought it was just one stalker?"

"Well, it—it is just the one stalker. But what if he's working with someone?"

Rick gave me a stern look. "Have you heard from him and not told me?"

"No," I answered quickly, as I shook my head. Technically, I was telling the truth. I'd only heard from Cynthia and Sean.

"And you would tell me if something was still happening, wouldn't you?"

I swallowed. "Of course. Of course, I would tell you."

"I'm serious, Chanelle. Is there anything you're not telling me?" Rick stared at me as though he were seeing through me.

His look was so intense, that I had to look away for a moment. I knew this was the perfect time to come clean. But Michele and I had worked out a plan, so I decided to keep quiet just a little longer. And once this nightmare had come to an end I would tell him everything. "Rick, there is nothing to tell you. The stalker hasn't reached out to me in weeks. Maybe he realized he had the wrong person." I gave a light laugh and put my hand on top of his.

He looked at me sideways. "Hmmm." He stood and pulled me up with him, holding my hand as we walked to the door. Before leaving, he kissed me and said, "I'm just a phone call away. Call me if you need me. And I have something to give you." He lifted his shirt, pulled his 9mm out of its holster and handed it to me.

I just stared at it, but didn't touch it. "Why are you giving me a gun?"

"Because you may need it. You said it yourself, you're a natural shot. And you passed your class with flying colors. I'm sure you won't need it, but just in case…"

I continued to stare at the weapon. "Thank you. But I'll be fine. I don't need a gun." I smiled and tried to reassure him.

"And you're probably right. But, if you do need it, I want to make sure you have it." He unclipped the holster from his belt, placed the gun back inside of it and laid it on the table by the front door.

He kissed me again and walked out, closing the door behind him.

❧

After Rick left, I dressed for bed and then called Michele.

"I don't know if this is a good thing or a bad thing, but Rick will be out of town for the next four days. He has a convention to attend for work."

"Are you scared?"

I was sitting cross-legged on my bed with the 9mm in front of me. "A little," I said, staring at the weapon. "But it's not like I've heard from anyone other than Sean for awhile. And if I look on the bright side, at least now I don't have to worry about Rick finding out what we're up to. I'm pretty sure we can bring this to a head and have it resolved before he returns. Are you all set for tomorrow?"

"Yes. I took BJ to my mother's for the week. And we're in the height of our busy season at work, so Ben will be working very late nights for the next month. He won't be home to ask me any questions."

"Perfect. Okay, I'm going in to work tomorrow and then I'll be by your house."

"Chanelle, it's not too late to change your mind."

"I know, but I can't live the rest of my life looking over my shoulder. One way or another, this ends. Soon."

"Somehow I knew you would say that."

"Thank you so much for doing this with me," I said with great sincerity.

"Yeah. Yeah. I really need to have my head examined."

I chuckled. "Your head is fine. I'll talk to you later." I hung up before she had a chance to say anything else.

I placed the gun in my nightstand drawer, then gave it some thought, and removed it from inside the drawer and placed it on top of the table, close to my bed. I said an extra prayer to God, and fitfully nodded off to sleep.

Michele and I were finally ready to begin Operation BAM, also known as "Operation By Any Means." Because I was going to get my life back, by any means necessary. If I hadn't already taken so much time off work, I wouldn't have gone in at all today. But I went in and did my best to focus. Around noon, Mr. Jeffries walked in.

"Hello, Chanelle. I'm glad I caught you. I'd like you to meet Lynelle. She's Sean's replacement." I looked behind Mr. Jeffries to see a curvy woman with long blond hair, olive skin, and dressed to perfection.

"Hello, Lynelle, it's nice meeting you."

"Likewise. Sean speaks very highly of you."

"Chanelle, would you mind bringing Lynelle up to speed on what you and Sean were working on?"

Yes, I mind. "Of course, Mr. Jeffries."

"Thank you," he said, then turned to her. "Lynelle, I'll be back in about an hour. And we can continue with our tour."

"Certainly, Mr. Jeffries," she said.

After the elderly gentleman left, I said, "So, tell me about yourself, Lynelle. How long have you been with Image?"

She began listing her pedigree, but all I could think about was the fact that it was my fault that Sean had lost his job. Well, it was his fault for whatever went down in Virginia. But it was my fault that Steve had looked into it.

I forced myself to listen to her ramble and was thrilled when Mr. Jeffries reappeared and took her from my office. I checked the clock every 10 minutes and as soon as the clock changed from 4:59 to 5:00, I grabbed my belongings, said a quick good bye to Patty, and scooted out the door.

As I stepped into the elevator, I called Michele. "I'm leaving now. I'll see you in about 15 minutes."

"Cool. I'll be ready."

"Were you able to make the calls we discussed?"

"Yup. I'll fill you in when you get here."

I said, "Okay," and pressed the 'off' button.

Twenty minutes later, she had her garage door up and I pulled in and parked next to her. She was already sitting in the driver's seat of her mom wagon, also known as the dreaded minivan. Before I could sit down, I had to brush animal crackers out of the front seat.

Michele started the engine. "Here." She handed me a large manila envelope as she backed out of the garage and hit the button in the van that closed the garage door.

As we headed down her street, I opened the envelope. "Wow! Your cousin, Elisa, got all this?"

"Yeah, and she said you can expect a bill in the mail. She put her job on the line to get you this info. Everything you have in your hands is hot off the presses. It was literally faxed to me right before you arrived." Michele merged onto the highway and pointed the car toward downtown.

I flipped through the pages. "I'll gladly pay it! How did she get all of this?"

"Well, you know she works for Speedy car rental and her boyfriend, Martin, works for a collection agency and he'll do anything for her. I gave her Cynthia's license plate number and we caught a lucky break. The car belongs to Speedy. So, she pulled up Cynthia's account and got the credit card number used to pay for the car. Then she gave the credit card number to Martin and he was able to get a report of all of Cynthia's transactions for the past 90 days. Judging by the report, she returned the car a day after you and Rick left for Aruba and she went home to Virginia. And it looks like she's been back and forth a handful of times, but most recently, she came back into town a few days ago. That's probably why Sean gave you a heads up call. Anyway, she rented from Speedy again. This time she has a white Malibu. The license plate number is in the fax. And she's staying at a Motel 8 near downtown, which is where we're going now."

I searched through the papers and found the license plate number. "Here it is. QWX495."

"This is our exit." Michele came off the freeway and made a few turns.

In moments, we had the Motel 8 in view. We backed into a space at the far end of the parking lot and scanned the area for the white Malibu.

"What's the number again?" Michele asked.

"QWX495."

"That might be it." She grabbed a pair of binoculars from her bag and pointed to a white car on the other side of the lot.

"Let me see." I snatched the binoculars from her hands and looked through the viewfinder. As the license plate number came into focus, a wide smile spread across my face. "That's it! We found her!"

"Don't get too thrilled. Remember, she's dangerous."

Michele's comments sobered my spirit and removed the smile from my face. "Right." I handed the binoculars back to her so she could see what I saw.

"What now?" she asked.

"Since we don't know which room is hers, we wait," I said. "We are officially on our first stake out. Did you bring any snacks? I haven't eaten since breakfast."

"I can do better than snacks." She reached into a cooler behind my seat and pulled out two turkey sandwiches, two bottles of water, and a big bag of chips.

"You're awesome! You keep your eyes on Cynthia's car and I'll go through the documents in the envelope," I said, while I unwrapped my sandwich and took a big bite.

"K. You must really be stressed and hungry. You didn't even bless your food before you attacked your sandwich."

"Oh, right. Thanks." I paused in mid-chew and took a moment to pray over my meal. Then I reviewed the packet and immediately noticed several charges to "GID Investigators".

"Hey, look at this." I showed Michele the papers. "This has to be the company that she hired. Although, I'm surprised he wouldn't be in a cash only business."

"Right. A hit man who takes credit? Doesn't he know paper trails are bad for his kind of business?"

"Apparently not. I wonder how we can find out—Look!" I cut myself off in mid-sentence. Cynthia was leaving her motel room. She dialed someone on her cell phone and then got into her car while still talking.

"Duck!" Michele shrieked. We both quickly slid down in our seats so Cynthia wouldn't see us as she drove past.

"Follow her!" I shouted. Michele dropped her sandwich, put the car in drive, and followed her out of the parking lot.

I was so anxious. I didn't want to lose her, but I also didn't want her to see us. "Slow down... Speed up... Switch lanes... She's gonna see you!" I yelled.

"Would you stop barking orders at me? You're being an awful backseat driver and you're making me nervous," Michele shot back.

"I'm sorry. I'll try and be quiet."

"Eat a chip and keep your mouth busy. I got this."

I shoveled potato chips in my mouth by the handful. Anything to keep myself from talking. We followed Cynthia for about 10 minutes until she finally pulled up in front of what looked to be an abandoned building in the middle of the block on a seedy side of town. She came to a stop behind an old dark colored Buick. We stopped at the end of block and watched for her next move.

"Michele, I think that's the same car the guy was driving the day I saw him at the gun range," I whispered.

"Maybe this is his office." She spoke so softly I could barely hear her.

Once again, we slid down in our seats. A scruffy looking man wearing a dingy white T-shirt, with a huge beer belly, and a cigar dangling from his lips, stepped from inside the building and surveyed the street. His eyes paused briefly on our van while he took a long drag on his cigar and scratched his stomach. We held our breath and prayed that he didn't see us. Thankfully, he turned his attention to Cynthia. He gave her a big hug and a swat on the butt, then the two of them walked inside.

"Now what?" Michele asked me.

"How should I know?"

"Well, you need to think of something quickly. Clearly they are still communicating with each other. This means that at this very moment they are plotting their next steps against you," she said, pointing at me.

"Don't you think I know that!"

"Don't yell at me. I'm in this with you. All I'm saying is we need to figure out what we're going to do next."

I backed down. "You're right. I'm sorry. I'm just on edge at the moment. I guess I didn't really think this through."

"You think?" she said very sarcastically.

"Just gimme a minute. I'll come up with something." I chewed on my thumbnail, contemplating what to do next. "Everything in me wants to know what they are talking about. We need a way inside that building without being seen."

"Any ideas on how we can do that? Because I'm all ears."

And then, as if a light bulb went off inside my head I said, "I got it! Let's wait until they leave and then break in and see what we can find. I bet he has a file on me. Maybe we can figure out what their next step is going to be."

Michele stared at me. "I swear I lost my best friend. Would you tell her I'm looking for her?"

"I'm serious, Michele."

"I am too. This is ludicrous. Let's call Steve."

"No. It's like Andrea said, I'm a punk if I don't get this under control on my own. And I'm nobody's punk. Steve took care of Sean for me. I can handle it from here. Besides," I said, pointing to the roof of the building, "it's only one story and it's flat. I remember years ago, I did a community center restoration project, kinda like Habitat for Humanity. Anyway, I learned that a lot of commercial buildings have ladders in the back that pull down. It's how contractors get onto the roof. And I'm sure we'll be able to find a way inside if we enter from the top."

Michele stared at me a little longer. "This is not an episode of Burn Notice. You are not Fiona. You are a corporate executive. The stuff you're talking about doing is crazy. For goodness sakes, you were never even a girl scout!"

"And neither were you."

"True. But I'm also not the one suggesting breaking into the building of a known stalker by climbing on the roof."

"Come on, Michele. We've already come this far. Let's just see it through to the end," I begged her.

After a silent standoff, Michele finally relented. "I'm sure I'll regret saying this, but fine."

"Thank you!" I gave her a big hug. "We'll need to go by your house so we can change clothes. I'm glad we wear the same size. Like you said, I'm corporate. There is no way I can climb onto that roof in my St. John suit," I said, referring to the outfit I was wearing.

"That's my point. You wore a St. John suit and Louboutin's to a stakeout. Why would you wear that anyway?"

I shrugged. "I dunno. I guess I wasn't thinking when I got dressed this morning."

"Mm-hmm. And now you want to climb on a roof."

"Yes. And finish my sandwich."

"Again, you're proving my point. We're snacking like we're on a picnic. Not watching the door waiting for a known killer to walk through."

"Michele, you say this like I don't realize that what is happening is very serious. Life and death. Because I do know that. I'm well aware of the risks I'm taking. And the risk I'm asking you to take with me. And you know I eat when I'm stressed. But please understand that I am taking this very seriously. Okay?"

Michele inhaled through her nose and exhaled slowly through her mouth. "Okay."

Michele and I watched the door for another hour. Finally, Cynthia emerged with the dirty looking man. We watched as he closed the front door behind them and locked it. Then we watched them each get into their respective vehicles. When they got to the corner, he went to the right and she went to the left.

"Which one should we follow?" Michele asked me.

"Well, we said we were going to go after Cynthia instead of him, so I guess, let's follow her."

Michele made a left and we tailed her to a liquor store and then back to her motel.

"Maybe she's in for the night," I said.

"We can only hope so."

"Let's head to your house so we can change."

She opened her mouth and then quickly closed it. I could only imagine the things that she wanted to say to me. But thankfully she decided to just support me and drive to her house.

"I'm glad Ben isn't home. The last thing I need to do is answer questions about my outrageous evening that isn't even over yet," Michele mumbled, as we pulled into her garage.

She wasn't really looking for a response, so I didn't offer one. We quickly changed into black leggings, black long sleeve turtle necks tops, black socks, and black boots. She had two hair scrunchies and we used them to pull our hair back.

As we got back into the minivan, I asked Michele if she had any mace and a flashlight.

"I believe so. Let me check." She went back inside the house and reappeared moments later with two cans of mace, two mini flashlights, a camera, and a small device I couldn't identify.

"Here," she said as she got in and handed me the items.

"What's this?" I asked her as I examined the gadget.

"It's a portable scanner. I typically use it for our business receipts, but I thought we might need it."

"Good idea!"

We chatted about trivial things, as we drove back to the stalker's office. Anything to keep our minds off of what we were about to do. All too soon, the abandoned looking building came into view. "Let's circle the block before we get out," I suggested.

"K."

Slowly we cruised around the block, our necks twisting around as we surveyed the area. When we didn't see any cars and we were confident that we were the only ones on the block, we parked across the street from the building. "You ready?" I asked.

"No. But I'm going to do it anyway."

Just as we were getting ready to step out of the van, I heard the sound of my ringtone. I dug my cell out of my purse and the caller ID said blocked. We looked at each other. We both knew it could only be one of two people.

"Should I answer?"

"Would you usually answer?"

I nodded. "Unfortunately, yes."

"Then answer."

I took a deep breath and placed the phone on speaker. "Hello?"

Chapter 37

"You know who dis is. You prollay thought you was done wit me, didn't cha?" Cynthia slurred.

Michele and I looked at each other again. "Cynthia, what are you talking about?"

"Don't play stupid wit me. Or maybe you ain't playin'. I know you went on yo' lil vacation to some island. I know yo' every move, you piece of trash. And when I said you was gonna pay, that's exactly what I meant. You gonna pay for what you did. And I know you the one behind Sean gettin' locked up."

I sighed. "Cynthia, what's happening between you and Sean is not my fault, including him being in jail."

"If you ain't have nothin' to do wit it, then how you know he in jail?"

I thought quickly. "For one, you just said it. And for two, I heard about it at work." Panic washed over me as I wondered if she'd say anything about Sean and me to Mr. Jeffries. "Look, I know I was wrong for what I did. But that was months ago. Whatever's going on between you two has nothing to do with me," I pleaded with her.

"You know, I always did hate you, but at least I used to think you was smart. But you dumb as a box of rocks because you believe what you sayin'. Don't you get it? Yeah, yeah, yeah, me and Sean, we had problems. But we coulda worked on it. After you came along, he changed his mind. He ain't wanna work on us no mo'. It's tricks like you, who think you can sleep with a woman's husband and then just walk away. Maybe I can't teach all tricks a lesson, but at least I can teach you a lesson. You crossed the line on me, and now I'm 'bout to cross the line on you." And with that, she hung up.

I leaned back in the seat and closed my eyes, trying to steady my breathing.

Michele gently took the phone from my hand and placed it on the console. "I know you wanted to 'flip the table' on her, as you put it. But I'm not so sure that we should approach her right now."

"Yeah. You're right. And before you tell me to call Steve, I'm going to remind you that I'm not. Because here's the thing, Michele. I want this to be over for good. I don't want to have to press charges against her for stalking and then have to deal with all the legal rigmarole. And that's exactly what I would have to do if I called Steve. He already told me that he only operates above board. So I'm calling on my inner Andrea and I'm handling this bit-," I caught myself and said, "chick myself. I don't know how this is going to play out, so if you want to back out, I'll understand."

"We agreed when we were kids that a real best friend is a ride or die best friend. We're ride or die to the end."

I looked at Michele. There were no words strong enough to explain how much I loved her. So I squeezed her hand and simply said, "Thank you."

"Come on. Let's do this."

We grabbed our items and dashed across the street to the backside of the building. As I anticipated, there was a ladder behind the building. We had to jump up to reach it, but after a few times, I was able to grab the bottom rung and I pulled it to the ground. Once on top of the roof, we looked for a way inside. In the far corner, we found a door and crossed our fingers that the door was unlocked. Unfortunately for us, it wasn't.

"Darn! Now what are we going to do?"

"Let's try this." Michele reached inside her pocket and pulled out two nail files.

"What are we supposed to do with those?"

"Pick the lock. We've seen it done on TV lots of times." Michele started wiggling the files around in the lock.

"Michele, this isn't TV. Do you know what you're doing?"

"How hard can it be? On TV they have the lock cracked in less than 30 seconds." Ten minutes later, she was still trying to get the lock open. "Boy, this is a lot harder than it looks on TV."

"Give it here. Let me see if I can do it."

"Gladly." She handed me the nail files and then I spent 10 minutes trying to open the lock. I brushed a few strands of hair out of my face. "Clearly, we need a new strategy." I looked around, but saw no other option.

"Maybe this is a sign that we shouldn't be doing this."

But I shook my head. "Nope. This is just a sign that we need to try harder." After another 20 minutes, I heard a click. "Yes!!" I turned the knob and the door opened. "Whew. Finally!!"

"You always were persistent."

I smiled. "Is there any other way to be? Let's see what we can find and get out of here."

I turned on my flashlight and we held hands, tiptoeing down the steps, which led to what appeared to be a maintenance room. On the other side of the room was another door. Once again I prayed that the door was unlocked and thankfully it was. I peeked my head out first and looked both ways down the narrow hall. There were no lights on, so I pointed my flashlight in the direction of the longer end of the hall and together we ventured out into the unknown. It was a small building and there were only four offices suites. "How are we supposed to know which is the right one?"

Michele looked to her right and said, "This has to be it." She pointed to a door that said, "Get It Done Investigators."

She tried turning the doorknob but, as expected, it was locked. "You got the other door open. I'm going to get this one open." And after 15 minutes, we heard the 'click'.

"Good job!" As we stepped inside the small office, I said, "Phew! It stinks in here." I gagged and covered my nose.

"What did you expect? You saw what he looked like." Michele searched for the light switch, but when she reached to turn it on, I grabbed her hand.

"Uh uh. Let's leave it off and use our flashlights."

"Good point," she agreed, turned on her little light, and walked over to the junky desk and started rifling through the papers on top. I followed the direction of my light and headed toward the old file cabinet behind the bureau.

A couple moments later, we both said, "I found something."

"You first," I told Michele and looked over her shoulder.

"He's been taking pictures of you. Look."

I stared in amazement at numerous pictures of myself. There had to be at least 75 photos. I picked them up and flipped through them. Me with Rick. Me with Michele. Me driving. Me in the parking garage at work. Rick and me at the gun range. Me at the grocery store.

"This is creepy. Did you bring in your camera?" When Michele nodded, I continued. "Let's spread them out and take pictures of the pictures." I fanned the photos on his desk and Michele began snapping. "Make sure you get pictures of his desk in the background."

"Got it."

As Michele took the pictures, I opened the file with my name that I'd found in the drawer. He had several notes of conversations that he'd had with Cynthia. The file was so thick that it was best to scan the pages and review them when we got back to Michele's. As I was scanning the last page, we heard footsteps in the hall and the sound of a man on the phone. We looked at each other and froze.

"Oh, my God," I said, my voice barely audible. "What are we gonna do?" We frantically looked around the room, but there was no decent place to hide.

"Under here." We immediately turned off our flashlights. I grabbed the file and scanner and Michele grabbed her camera and we hid in the small space under his desk. The footsteps drew closer and then came to a stop in front of the door.

Slowly the doorknob turned and the door cracked open. "Humph. I could've sworn I locked the door," we heard him say.

I trembled and said a silent prayer. "Oh Lord, if you love me, please protect me."

He flipped on the light and turned his attention back to his conversation. "Cynthia, I told you I got this." He paused while she spoke. "Yeah, yeah. I'll have this wrapped up by the end of the week." Another pause. "No, nothing will blow back on you." In a few short steps, he was standing in front of his desk.

I looked at the floor and his beat up loafers came into view. My heart stopped.

We heard him sift through the papers on his desk and grab what sounded like a set of keys. Then he turned and headed back to the door. "If you want me to kill her, I'll kill her. Don't make me no difference. The fee is the same." The light switched went off and he closed and locked the door behind him. It wasn't until we heard the sound of his retreating footsteps that we exhaled.

"Let's get out of here," I said.

Michele waited while I re-scanned the final page and returned the file to the drawer. Then we cautiously exited the office, remembering to lock it behind ourselves. I turned to go back the way we came in, but Michele grabbed my arm. "Wait. Why not leave through the front door?"

I paused. "What if there's some alarm on it? I say we go back the way we came."

"Ok," she said.

We made a beeline for the maintenance room, raced each other back up the steps, through the door, onto the roof, and down the ladder. We didn't slow down until we were safely inside the van. Michele gunned the motor and sped back to the safety of our side of town.

Chapter 38

"This is like the night that just won't end," Michele moaned. It was well after 2:00 in the morning and we'd been in her basement for a couple hours going through the documents that we'd copied.

When Ben arrived home about an hour earlier, he took one look at the Chinese dinner cartons, our outfits, and all the papers on the floor, said he didn't want to know what we were up to, and went to bed.

"I know and I'm exhausted." I took a long sip of my Pepsi and stretched my arms. Much of the information we had only confirmed what we already knew. Cynthia blamed me for the breakdown of her marriage and was determined to make me pay. She'd responded to an ad on Craigslist and that's how she found this guy. She'd paid him $1500 to taunt me and right around the time Sean was arrested, she paid him an additional $500 for what he referred to as "investigator discretion." As far as we could tell, that meant he could do whatever he wanted, up to and including death.

"You know, I think I'm going to call Steve tomorrow," I said. "This is bigger than I can handle. Andrea is just going to have to call me a punk. At least I'll be a punk who's alive."

"That's the first smart thing you've said in months!"

I rolled my eyes and pursed my lips at my best friend. "I hate it when we have these 'I told you so' moments."

"We've both had a very long and exhausting day. How about we put this away for now and look at it with a fresh eye tomorrow before you talk to Steve?"

I yawned. She had a point. I was so tired, I was seeing double. "Okay. But I'm still going into the office. If my attendance doesn't improve, Mr. Jeffries is liable to rescind my partnership," I half joked.

"He wouldn't do that. You're too valuable to him. Are you going home in the morning before you head in?"

"Yes. I certainly can't go in wearing this get up." I pointed to the all-black outfit I had borrowed. I headed toward her spare bedroom in the basement. "Good night." I was sound asleep almost before my body hit the mattress and my head hit the pillow.

"Wake up! Chanelle, wake up!" In my haze I felt someone shaking me. "Wake up. It's 9:00. You're late."

"Huh?" I willed my eyes to open. I was so exhausted.

"Get up! You still have to get home and get dressed."

"Home?"

"Yes. You're at my house. Remember, you spent the night?"

Slowly, Michele came into focus and the events of yesterday replayed in my mind. "Oh, no! I'm late!" I sprang out of bed and hunted around for my shoes.

"That's what I've been trying to tell you for the last 5 minutes."

I was frantic. "No. No. No. I can't be late. Do you have anything I can wear?"

"Of course I do. Hop in the shower and I'll find something for you." Michele sprinted out of my room and I grabbed a washcloth and towel from the bathroom closet and took the quickest shower in history. Fortunately, I was a regular overnight guest at her house and kept an overnight kit in her spare bedroom, so my morning routine wasn't too disrupted. When I stepped back into the bedroom, Michele had placed a black pantsuit and new underwear on the chair. I dressed, did my makeup, slipped on a pair of her heels, and was out the door and pulling into the parking lot at work in less than 35 minutes.

"Good morning, Patty," I said as I breezed by her and headed toward my office.

"Hey, Boss Lady. You just missed Rick's call."

I stopped cold in my office doorway and turned to face Patty. "Rick called?"

"Yeah. I told him you weren't in yet. Then he asked me the strangest thing."

"Wha—what did he ask?"

"He asked me how my old man was doing."

"Oh. Um, wha—what did you tell him?" I tried to ask nonchalantly.

"I was a little puzzled because I thought it was odd that he was asking 'bout my man, but I told him he's doin' good."

"And was that the entire conversation?" I prayed she would say yes.

"No. Then he asked how I was doin' and he was sorry to hear that my old man had to go to the hospital after gettin' hurt at work."

"Oh. And then wha- what did you say?"

"Well, then I figured out that you must've used me as some sort of cover story. And I don't wanna know what you was tryin' to cover because it ain't my business. So I said we is all doin' fine and thanks for askin'. Boss Lady, I don't care if you need to use me. Just in the future, please tell me. Okay? I can do a much better job if I have a heads up."

I smiled and relaxed. I could always count on Patty to have my back. "Yes. I'm so sorry, Patty. I promise I won't put you in that position again. Thank you so much!"

"Anytime, Boss Lady. Anytime. Also, Mr. Jeffries added a meeting on your calendar for this morning. You got about 5 minutes."

"Thanks," I said. She turned and went back to working on her computer and I went inside my office, dropped off my bags, then went to the break room to fix a cup of coffee before I going to my meeting.

The meeting was brief, and within an hour I was on my way back to my office. My plan was to call Steve and set up a time to meet after work, and then call Rick. But when I got to my suite, Patty said, "Hey Boss Lady, you have a visitor. I figured it'd be okay if he waited in your office."

I frowned. She knew it was a no-no to leave people in my office without my permission, but when I opened my door, I understood why she did it. "Rick! What are you doing here?" I said, closing the door behind me, then walking over and embracing him.

"We didn't talk yesterday and I missed you."

"Awww. I missed you, too."

He hugged me back, then handed me a bouquet of red roses.

"You spoil me! These are beautiful, but what are you doing here? You're supposed to be in Chicago."

He sat down on the couch and motioned for me to sit next to him, which I did, still holding my flowers. "I couldn't concentrate. I called your house for hours last night and you never answered. I got worried, so I drove back this morning. Where were you? And why didn't you answer your phone?"

"Oh. I spent the night at Michele's. Ben is working late this week, so we had girl-bonding time. Nothing special. We do it often when they are in the middle of their peak season. Why didn't you call my cell?"

"I did. It went straight to voicemail."

"I never heard it ring." I got up, placed my flowers on my desk, and reached inside of my purse for my phone. It was dead. "See." I showed him the blank screen. "I didn't realize it was off." I placed it on the charger and returned to my seat next to him.

"Um-hmm." Rick paused. "Chanelle, I'm going to ask you something and I want you to give me a straight answer."

"I'm always straight with you."

"No, you're not. I feel like you're keeping something from me."

"What makes you say that?"

"Just a feeling I have. I can't do lies. If we're going to work, we have to have complete and total honesty with each other. Don't you agree?"

"Of course."

"Then tell me what you're hiding."

"I—I'm not hiding anything."

His body tensed and his jaw tightened. "I know you're lying to me. So I'm going to ask you one last time. What. Are. You. Hiding?"

I bit the inside of my lip, rubbed the back of my neck, and picked at imaginary lint on my suit. So many things ran through my mind. He was right. I had to be honest and let the chips fall wherever they were going to fall. After about 60 seconds of deafening silence, I mumbled, "I know who's stalking me and I know why."

"What?" he yelled and jumped up.

"Shhh! Lower your voice, please." I patted the seat, but he continued to stand.

"Who is doing this to you and why didn't you tell me? And when did you find out?" His voice remained at the same extra loud volume.

"Please lower your voice. I'll tell you everything. Promise." I patted the seat again and this time he sat back down, but on the edge. I reached for his hand, but he pulled away from me.

"Talk."

I had seen this side of Rick once before when we were in college. I could feel the clouds hovering over me and there was nothing I could do to stop the torrential downpour that was coming my way.

So, I just started talking. "Several months ago, before you came back into my life, I had a brief, very brief, affair with a married man. I knew he was married and I knew it was wrong, but I did it. Anyway, he and his wife moved away and that was it. I moved on with my life and he did, too. Or so I thought. But then he called me. He told me that he was coming to Michigan and that he wanted to see me. I told him no and that I had moved on. That's when I found out who was behind the dead rat and the phone calls. Apparently he told his wife about us and said he wanted a divorce. They were already going through problems. I'm pretty sure she was doing her own thing on the side, but that's irrelevant to her. She blames me for her situation getting worse and she hired someone to threaten me."

I put my head down because I couldn't bear to look at him, but I could feel the steam coming off his body. "How long have you known?"

"For a while."

"What's 'a while'?"

"Ummm… since before our vacation."

"What?" he yelled and jumped up again. "And you found out how, again?" He began pacing back and forth.

I repeated what I had said just seconds earlier. "Her husband called me. He told me that he's in love with me and asked if we could meet. I said no and that I'd moved on."

He stopped pacing long enough to stand over me and glower. "And that day when we were sitting on the couch, and you said the office was on phone?"

"That was Sean; he's the husband. He was telling me that he was moving back to Michigan."

"Wait. Sean? Is that the guy who was in your office on your first day back? The guy who I said looked like he was more than just a coworker."

I was forced to nod.

"Mm-hmm. And that day in the kitchen. When you said Patty's husband had been in an accident?"

"That wasn't true. I had just received a call from him again. He was calling me from jail and telling me that his wife blamed me for him being arrested."

"Arrested? Why was he arrested?"

"Um," I began. I didn't want to tell the truth, but I'd come this far. No need to hold back now. The chips were already falling. "He'd made it clear that he didn't care that I was happily involved with you. He said he wasn't giving up on us. I talked to Steve, Michele's brother, and asked if there was anything he could do to help me. Turns out, Sean had a warrant for his arrest and Steve executed the warrant. He's been taken back to Virginia to stand trial or whatever. But he called me from jail and told me to watch my back."

"Let me make sure I understand. You've known for weeks who was responsible for the threats against you. And you didn't trust me enough to tell me?"

"It's not like that," I said. "I did trust you. I do trust you. I was just worried that you would judge me and I didn't want you to leave. You were adamant about faithfulness and I didn't know how to tell you that I'd made a mistake. I didn't want to lose you. I needed you. I need you. I am sorry that I kept this from you."

The volume of his voice had returned to normal, but he was still seething with anger. "So am I, Chanelle. So am I. You looked me in my face and lied to me. Not once. Not twice. But multiple times. You know, people make mistakes all the time. And I understand that you could get caught up and make some bad choices. I would've never passed judgment on you for what you did with her man. But what I don't think I can ever forgive is lying to me. If I can't trust you, then I can't be with you. And right now, I can't trust you." He turned away from me and marched toward the door.

I bounced up and ran after him. "Rick, I'm sorry. Please don't leave. Please stay." I grabbed his arm, but he shook me off.

"I'm sorry too, Chanelle. I'm sorry that you aren't the woman I thought you were. Goodbye." And with that he turned and walked out of the door. And walked out of my life.

Chapter 39

I plopped down in my desk chair and looked outside my window at the beautiful skyline and for the millionth time, I told myself that this was not my life. Pastor Sharpe's warning to me before I took it too far with Sean played in my mind: *it won't end well.* And she was correct. I always knew that decisions have consequences, but I never expected this. I closed my eyes, pinched the bridge of my nose, and sighed. Staying at work was useless. I grabbed my items, told Patty that I wasn't feeling well, and left.

I was so immersed in my sorrow that I forgot to call Steve. I stopped at Chipotle and got a vegetarian burrito bowl and lemonade to go. Within moments, I was home and sitting in my den, mindlessly flipping through the channels. I settled on a court TV program and made a futile attempt at enjoying my lunch.

After about an hour, I picked up my home phone on the table next to the couch and dialed Rick. It rang a couple times and then I heard instructions to leave a message.

Wow, I never expected him to push me to voicemail. I left him a rambling apology and hung up. This was even worse than

I thought. I tried to re-dial his number, but I got a busy signal when I clicked the 'on' button. I clicked the phone off and tried again. Same busy signal. I set the phone down and reached for my cell phone in my purse. Before I had a chance to process why my phone had suddenly stopped working, I heard the sound of my front door opening. I panicked momentarily until I remembered that Rick had a key.

"Rick? Is that you?" I leaped from the couch and raced to the foyer. But I stopped in my tracks when I realized that I wasn't looking at Rick. I was looking at the dirty looking grungy man that Cynthia had hired. I was looking at The Stalker.

"Naw, I ain't Rick. I'm Brutus. And it's time we had a little chat."

He was as wide as a wall, and he was blocking my escape through the front door. I immediately looked at the hall table and my heart sank when I remembered that the gun Rick had given me was upstairs in my bedroom.

As he moved toward me, I backed up and then took off running to my bedroom with him right behind me. As I reached the top of the stairs, he caught my leg, causing me to fall, and the carpet burned the side of my face as my head bounced down the steps. I struggled to catch the banister for leverage and kicked him off me. He fell backwards to the bottom, giving me time to regain my balance and dash to my room. And my sidearm.

I slammed and locked the door behind me and ran to my nightstand. With shaking hands, I reached for my gun. But before I had a chance to snatch it, my door flew open and Brutus clutched me from behind and threw me to the other side of my California king-size bed. I screamed.

"Things will go much smoother if you stop fightin'," he growled, coming toward me.

Pouncing on top of me, he pinned my arms over my head and bent down to kiss me. Twisting my head from side to side I did my best to avoid his chapped lips from touching my face, but when it looked like it was inevitable, I spit in his eyes.

"You're gonna pay for that!" he bellowed, punching me in my face. I felt like the jagged bone fragments from my busted nose had traveled up my nasal cavity and pierced my brain. Blood immediately pooled in my mouth and I had to turn my head to the side so I wouldn't drown in my own fluid.

He grabbed the bottom of my shirt and wiped his face, then punched me harder than a boxer in the ring, this time darkening my eye.

"Get off me!" I mustered up as much strength as I had to push him away, but he was a man possessed and was immovable.

"Stop fightin'. Can't nobody hear ya and you just makin' things harder for ya self." He sat up enough to adjust his straddle over me and re-pin my arms above my head. While he fixed himself, I saw the opportunity to knee him in his most private part. "Arrgh!" he yelped and grabbed his wounded jewels.

I took advantage of the moment and kicked him one more time. As he doubled over, I flew off the bed and ran around to the other side, back to my nightstand. I once again reached for my gun and this time I was successful. With blood dripping into my eyes, I cocked the trigger and pointed it at him.

"Now, who's gonna pay? Put your hands behind your back and get up."

He began rising slowly, then lunged toward me, reaching for the gun to snatch it from my trembling hands. As I jerked back and out of his reach, the gun slipped from my fingers, firing into the wall behind him and sliding underneath the bed.

We fell to the ground, both of us scrambling to be the one to retrieve the weapon. I grabbed the gun just as he yanked my legs, flipped me on my back and dragged me toward him. He got back on top of me, with the gun between us.

Each time he slammed my head into the floor, I lost a little more consciousness. I knew I only had mere seconds before I blacked out. I squeezed my eyes shut, exactly the way I had been taught not to do it, and pulled the trigger.

Bang!

The pounding of my head into the floor stopped and for the second time that day, he fell to his side and off of me.

I heard a blood curdling scream. "Chanelle!!"

"Michele?" I answered weakly, and then I passed out.

Chapter 40

"Where am I?" I moaned, only able to look around the room with my eyes because my head felt like it was anchored to my pillow.

"Welcome back, Ms. Slate. You're at First General Hospital." An elderly woman in a nurse's uniform smiled down at me. "You had us scared for a moment."

"Wha- what happened? Why am I here?"

"You were in a very bad fight. Lucky for you, your friend saved your life." She nodded in the direction of Michele, who was sleeping in the visitor's chair in my hospital room. "She's been by your side since you arrived."

"How long have I been here?"

"Four days. You were in a coma for the first few days, but you started coming around yesterday."

"A coma?"

"Mm-hmm."

"Ooh," I groaned. "I feel like my face is about to pop off."

"That's natural. I just changed your morphine drip, so you should feel some relief soon."

"Was the rest of my family here?"

"They've all been in and out. But that lady right there," she said, pointing at Michele, "she never left."

I tried to sit up but felt a sharp pain shoot through my head and screamed out in pain.

"Chanelle?" Michele said, jumping up and hurrying to my bedside. "You're awake! Oh, my God! You had me so worried." She leaned over the side rail of the bed and gently kissed my forehead.

"Lay back, Ms. Slate," the nurse said in an overly soothing tone. "You'll feel best if you try not to move. The doctor will be in shortly and she'll be able to give you more info." She placed a remote next to my hand. "Here's the call button. Use it if you need to reach me." She gave Michele a reassuring pat on her shoulder and left the room.

"Can you tell me what happened?"

Her eyes clouded over. "You don't remember anything?"

"Not much."

"Well, you were attacked in your home. Do you remember that?"

I closed my eyes and tried to think back. "Kinda. I remember leaving work early… I think Rick and I had an argument." I paused. "Yes, we had an argument. He said I wasn't honest with him." I paused again as images of the day began to play in my mind. "I left work early, grabbed some lunch, and went home… I called Rick but he didn't answer. I heard my front door open and thought it was Rick, but it wasn't him. It was…" I gasped as the rest of my memories came flooding back to me. "The stalker. The stalker was in my home! We fought and… the gun. It went off!"

"I don't know how to tell you this, but…" Before she could finish her sentence my hospital room door opened and two men, with badges hanging from a chain around their necks, walked in.

The senior of the two greeted me. "Hello, Ms. Slate. I'm Detective Watson and this is my partner Detective Brunson. If you're feeling up to it, we'd like to have a word with you." Both men approached my bed.

"Sure. They tell me I just woke up from a coma, so please excuse me if I'm a little groggy." In my hazy frame of mind, I was still pretty sure that it was too soon for detectives to be questioning me.

"Understandable. Understandable. All we need you to do is tell us what you remember about your incident."

"It's slowly coming back to me, but I'll tell you what I can." I recounted the information that I had just shared with Michele, including the details of the fight that I could recall.

"And that's it? You don't remember anything else?" the younger detective asked me.

"I'm sorry. I don't."

"Did you realize that you shot Mr. Cowan?"

"Mr. Cowan? Who's Mr. Cowan?"

"Mr. Brutus Cowan. He's the gentleman who was in your home."

I felt some of my sass returning to me or maybe it was the morphine. "If you're referring to the pervert who stalked me and later assaulted me in my home, then you're not speaking of a gentleman. And to answer your question, no, I do not recall shooting him. At least not specifically. He was on top of me, pounding my head into the floor, and the gun was between us. I do recollect hearing the gun go off, but I couldn't tell you if he got shot or if I did."

"That was when I got there and saw her on the carpet next to her bed," Michele interjected.

The officers turned to face Michele. "And you are?" Detective Watson inquired.

"I'm Mrs. Michele Burke, Chanelle's best friend. And I'm the one who found her nearly unconscious, and half dead, on the floor."

"Please go on." Detective Watson had out his little notepad and was feverishly writing down Michele's statement.

"To back up just a little, I called Chanelle's office and her assistant told me she'd left early. She thought Chanelle and her boyfriend had gotten into an argument and Chanelle seemed distraught. I figured she would've gone home, so I went by to check on her. I have a key to her house and let myself in. That's when I heard some sort of commotion coming from upstairs. I ran up the steps to her bedroom and I saw Cowan on top of her, banging her head into the floor. Next thing I knew, I heard a gunshot, he fell over, and she passed out. I called 911 and the EMS brought her here. I have no idea what ended up happening to him. For the record, I gave my statement to the police officer who was here a couple days ago while Chanelle was still in a coma."

"Yes, we're aware of that Mrs. Burke. However, since Mr. Cowan has now died, this case has been turned over to homicide."

"He died?"

"Yes, Ms. Slate," Detective Watson said. "Mr. Cowan passed away this morning. It's our job to determine if this is a case of homicide or self-defense. Do you have any idea why he was in your home? Did you know him? Earlier you referenced that he was stalking you?"

"Yes, he was stalking me."

"Do you know why? And did you report it to the police?"

I was silent for a moment. I knew I needed to tell the truth, but really, how much of the truth did they need to know? The whole truth would include breaking and entering into Cowan's office, illegally obtained credit documents, an affair with someone else's husband, and utilizing Steve to help get Sean arrested. I could get innocent people in trouble. And I could also come off looking as guilty as Cowan and Cynthia. I had to choose my words very carefully. I cleared my throat, praying that the medication wouldn't make me say something I was trying to keep to myself. "Well, I didn't notify the police because he told me that he would hurt my family."

"And do you know why he was stalking you, as you put it? Were you in a relationship with him?"

"Absolutely not!" I quickly answered. And then hesitated. It was unbelievable that a foolish decision on my part several months ago was having such an awful ripple effect. Here I was, laid up in a hospital bed with traumatic injuries, answering questions about a murder that I had just committed. A murder! Me! There was no way all of this was happening to me!

I took a deep breath. Here goes nothing, I thought. "I dated a married man months ago. His wife blamed me for the breakdown of their marriage. She hired Cowan to harass me. He told me that killing me was not out of the question. He broke into my house, we fought, and apparently I shot him." There. I told the truth.

Detective Brunson unconsciously touched his wedding band and I felt like I should've had a scarlet letter branded on my hospital gown. "How do you know his wife blamed you? Can you prove any of what you're saying?"

Of course I can prove it, I thought. But how do I prove it without getting myself into trouble? "I know she blamed me because she called me and told me. Her husband also warned me that she was out to get me." I suddenly remembered that Sean had left me a message to be careful. "And I saved the voicemail from her husband if you'd like to hear it." I knew at the end of the message he said he loved me and I was sure that I would get a strange look from the detectives, but this was my life I was fighting to keep.

"Yes, we'd like to hear that if you have it."

I looked to Michele. "Do I have my cell phone?"

She shook her head. "It's at your house. And your house has been taped off as a crime scene."

I looked back to the detectives. "If you can get to my cell phone, you'll hear my proof."

"Do you have anything else?" Detective Brunson asked.

I thought hard and then said, "My assistant! My assistant was there when Cowan first called me." I gave him Patty's contact information.

"And is there anything else?"

"Well…" I hedged. "Um, he has an office on Third and Cass. I believe it's called 'Get It Done Investigators'. I'm sure he has a file with my name on it."

Detective Watson squinted his eyes and furrowed his brows. "You're sure there's a file, huh?"

I looked as sweet and innocent as I could. "Uh-huh. And that file will probably have notes on who put the hit out on me. If you can find that, then that would clear my name, right? And maybe you could even arrest Cynthia." I tried batting my eyelashes at him, but they seemed to be almost swollen shut.

"One step at a time. We're going to follow up with the leads you've provided. *If* what you're saying is true, then the Castle Law would apply and you would not be charged with first-degree murder. But don't leave town when you're released from the hospital. We'll be in touch soon. Get well." And with that, the detectives turned and left the room.

"Michele, what if they come back and say that I committed cold-blooded murder? You don't think that would happen, do you?"

"Of course not! I saw what was happening to you. He was literally beating you to death. I'm sure that everything will all work out. I'll be back in a moment. I think it was too soon for the detectives to come and question you and I'm going to make sure that no one else comes in for the rest of the day."

She left to find the doctor and I did my best to find sleep. My head was pounding, my heart was racing. I was scared and I really wanted Rick. No, I needed Rick. He probably didn't even know what had happened to me. I couldn't imagine him knowing and not being here.

Michele returned with the doctor, who gave me an update on my condition. Though I had been badly injured, none on my injuries were life-threatening. There was slight swelling on my brain, but no permanent damage. Even though my nose would have to be fixed, the doctor was hopeful I would be released within a week, two at the most. That news was the first comforting thing I'd heard all day. She turned up my morphine dose so I could sleep and within moments I was sleeping like a newborn baby.

Chapter 41

"Home sweet home."

"Kinda," I responded with a slight smile and slowly stepped inside my front door into the foyer. I'd ended up staying in the hospital for 2 weeks, but I'd finally been released with minimal home care instructions.

Yesterday, the crime scene tape had been removed and I was free to return to my residence, though it would be another couple of days before the carpet company could come out and replace my bedroom flooring. Thankfully, the police had checked into everything and determined that I was telling the truth. After returning to the hospital to question me several more times over the past week, they were confident that I had been stalked and that Cynthia was behind it. They recommended to the DA that no charges be filed against me and instead they went after Cynthia. I was so relieved.

I received a call this morning from Detective Watson that Cynthia was picked up last night. They fully expected her to be charged with conspiracy to commit murder. Apparently, in addition to the files and pictures that Michele and I discovered, Cowan also recorded phone calls with Cynthia that Michele and

I had overlooked. Lucky for me, the detectives never asked me again how I knew about Cowan's office and his files and I never volunteered that information.

"My mom has been keeping BJ for me, but she's going on a cruise with the ladies from church and I need to swing by there and pick him up. I'll be back after I get him settled at home with Ben."

"No, Michele. You have been away from your family much too much over these last few weeks because of me. Go home. Spend some quality time with your family. I'll be fine."

Michele looked skeptical. "Are you sure? I feel really funny about leaving you home alone. Why don't you come home with me? At least until they finish cleaning your room."

I shook my head. "Uh uh. I'll be fine. I'm feeling okay. I have almost a clean bill of health. No charges were filed against me. Cowan is gone. Sean is gone. Cynthia's been arrested. This is the best I've felt in a long time. I may be moving a little slowly, but I feel like I'm on top of the world." I paused and thought about the hole I felt in my heart. "The only thing that would make this day better is Rick. But I guess he really meant it when he said he couldn't forgive me."

On the one hand, there were no words to describe how elated I was that my nightmare was over. On the other, I was filled with a sadness unlike anything I'd ever felt before because I hadn't heard from the man who made me the happiest I had ever been in my life. I missed his smile and his comforting arms. I missed his companionship. And most of all, I just missed him.

Instead of feeding into my pity party, Michele admonished me. "He would have been there for you if you'd simply called him and told him what was going on." She set my bags down in the living room, then headed to the kitchen to make me a cup of tea, while I stretched out in my recliner.

I had never been one to beg a man for anything, but I was so wrong in this instance that I was willing to humble and humiliate myself to win Rick back.

Michele returned with a steaming hot cut of chamomile tea. "Here you go. Everything will be fine. You get some rest and I'll call you later." She paused to look at me and her eyes began to tear. "I'm so happy you're okay. I don't know what I would have done without my best friend."

"Don't go gettin' all sentimental. You know I'm on too much medication right now. You'll have me cryin' and I won't be able to stop." I tried to chuckle as I looked at my bestie. But I was overcome with emotion. "You are the best friend I have in the world. Every woman needs a ride or die and I'm so blessed that you're mine."

Michele bent down and gave me the biggest, warmest hug I'd had in a long time. And I needed it. The floodgate of tears that I'd been holding in since the day I was taken to the hospital was finally unleashed. And I cried for what felt like hours. "I love you, girl."

"I love you too, my sister from another mister." I said the phrase that we'd been saying to each other since high school.

"Let me get going." She dabbed her eyes with a tissue on the coffee table. "I'll check in a little later."

"Thanks for everything."

"Anytime." She turned the corner and walked out the door.

I breathed a little easier when I heard the sound of the door lock. I looked around the room and that's when it hit me that the last time I was in my home, I'd been attacked.

I got up and grabbed my cup of tea and walked to the foot of my steps. I stood there for a moment and looked to the top. My eyes landed on the step where I'd been caught and dragged backwards. I brought my hand to my face and touched the remains of my carpet burn. I felt my heart speed up and I had to take a few deep breaths to steady myself. I needed to see my bedroom.

One step at a time, I walked up my stairs, which felt like the long green mile. I felt a sense of accomplishment when I reached the top, and then I looked at my bedroom door. Everything in my body paused. My heart. My breathing. My everything.

"You can do this, Chanelle. You can do this. Count to 3 and open the door." Silently I counted and slowly turned the door handle.

As soon as my room came into view, images of my terror flashed through my mind like a trailer to a horror movie. I saw me being thrown on the bed, fighting for my life. Being punched in the face. Struggling with him over the gun.

I walked over to the side of my bed where Cowan had met his fate. I almost passed out when I saw the chalk outline of his body. I immediately placed my hand over my mouth and took in large gulps of air in an attempt to keep my breakfast down. I had never seen a crime scene before, but this was not what I pictured. I had second thoughts about not going home with Michele and either I was going to take her up on her offer or sleep downstairs until my bedroom was repaired.

I quickly turned and shuffled out of the room, slamming the door shut behind me. I made it back down the steps as quickly as my injured body would take me.

As I reached the bottom step, my doorbell rang. The only person who knew I was back home was Michele and she had a key. I peered out the peephole and my heart skipped a beat.

It was Rick.

"Hi." I spoke softly.

"Baby, what happened?" he said, reaching out to softly touch my face when he saw my nose splint and still bruised eyes.

"I met the stalker. He lost."

"Oh my God, Chanelle. Are you okay?"

I nodded.

"May I come in?"

I hadn't realized he was still standing on the other side of the door frame. "Oh yes, please." I stepped aside so he could enter. After closing the door, we just stood awkwardly, neither of us knowing what to say next.

"Please tell me what happened."

I nodded again. "Follow me. Would you like something to drink?"

"Sure. What are you drinking?" he asked, referring to the cup in my hand.

"Michele just left and she fixed me a cup of chamomile tea. Would you like some?"

"That would be great." He followed me into the kitchen and sat at the kitchen table. The water was still hot, so I grabbed a tea bag and steeped it in a mug. I added honey and ginger, just the way I knew he liked it.

"Here you go." I placed the mug in front of him and sat in the chair across from him.

"Thank you."

More awkward silence.

"Chanelle. What happened?"

I took a deep breath and told him the events of my last 2 weeks.

"Baby, I'm sorry I wasn't there for you. That I let a stupid argument stop me from protecting you."

"Rick, it's okay. You couldn't have known. So, what brings you by anyway?" I inquired.

"I missed you," he said simply. "I thought it would be easy to walk away from you and it wasn't. I'm very disappointed in you, Chanelle, but I'm not ready to throw away what we were building. I love you too much."

My heart did backflips. "I love you and I missed you, too. And I'm so very, very sorry for not being straight with you. I was scared to lose you and by keeping things from you I almost did. I truly, truly, truly apologize. Will you please forgive me?"

"Of course I forgive you. But you have to promise me something."

"You name it and I'll promise it." I smiled at him.

"No more lies. One hundred percent honesty between us from now on. Can you promise that?"

"Yes. I will always tell you the truth. And I'll start now." I confessed everything. I began with how Sean and I met and I stopped right before I retold him about Cowan breaking into my house. I saw Rick hold back a laugh as I told him about our adventure on top of the roof. Now that I was safe and no longer in danger, I had to agree that it was a little humorous.

"I'm so sorry I wasn't there for you," he said again.

"I know you would have been if our situation had been different at the time. But what's important is that you're here now."

"And I'm not ever leaving you. I mean that." He got up and walked over to me. He gently pulled me up and held me close.

For the second time that day, I got the best hug in the world. Only his came with a slow gentle kiss. And for the first time in my life, everything was right with my world...

Epilogue

It had been six months since my ordeal came to an end. I had to testify at Cynthia's trial, which I did gladly. She got a 15-year sentence for conspiracy to commit murder. I saw Sean at her trial. Mr. Jeffries told me he'd been cleared of all charges, but he'd decided to stay in Virginia and build a life there. He'd only been at her trial to see how much time she'd receive. Apparently, she'd been behind the embezzlement case and was going to have to stand trial in Virginia when this case was over.

I was finally back on track at work and Mr. Jeffries was happy to have 100% of me. Patty was still complaining about all of her aches and pains and her crazy family. Michele was back to spending time at home with her family now that my shenanigans had come to an end.

Andrea was still Andrea. About a week after I returned home, I invited her over for dinner and updated her on my life. She feigned sympathy and then asked for a loan. Like I said, Andrea was still Andrea.

My bedroom and master bath were completely redone, compliments of Rick. It had taken about a month for us to truly put the past behind us, but we did it. And now we were in a very peaceful place. I was sure that my engagement was on the horizon.

"Hey, Sweetie," Rick said as he met me out on the deck where I was grilling some salmon and asparagus.

"Hey, Babe." I greeted him with a quick kiss. "Dinner is almost ready, so go wash your hands."

"Yes ma'am," he joked and set his sunglasses and phone on the table before heading inside to wash his hands.

As he walked out back into the house, his phone rang. "Babe, would you grab that?"

Still smiling, I said, "I got it." I glanced at the caller ID and it said "unknown."

"Hello?"

"Who is this?" a female voice asked me.

"Who is this?" I responded with my own question.

"This is Rick's wife, Twyla."

I was taken aback. "Excuse me, but don't you mean his ex-wife?" I corrected her.

"Once a wife, always a wife. Now is Rick there? Because I want to speak with my husband," she demanded.

Was she serious? "My man is unavailable at the moment, but I'll tell him you called. Would you like to leave a message?"

"Humph. Yeah, as a matter of fact I do. You tell him that we ain't over. I'm comin' back to take what's mine. He knows the number. Have him call me." And she hung up before I had a chance to respond.

"Babe, who was on the phone," Rick asked as he came up behind me, wrapped his arms around me, and nuzzled my neck.

I turned to face him. "That was your ex-wife. She said to call her. She wants you back." I handed him his cell and walked out of the room.

He was speechless and in an instant, I saw the peace of my life shatter. I had a feeling I would be calling Michele later that evening. I had a problem and she was the only one I trusted to help me fix it.

Bad Choices Can Be Deadly

Book Club Guide

1. Michele was Chanelle's bestie. She was Chanelle's voice of reason and yet Michele was also in her corner from beginning to end. Do you have a ride or die bestie that always has your back? Discuss.

2. Chanelle was very successful at work, but her personal life started out a mess. How is it that a woman can be put together professionally and in control of her career and yet her personal life is so out of control?

3. If Chanelle's boss, Mr. Jeffries, found out about her relationship with Sean, do you think she should have been fired? Discuss your reason for your answer.

4. So many women want a man like Rick. A man who steps up and takes care of her when she's in need. Discuss the characteristics that showed that Rick was a good, strong man.

5. Cynthia was obviously a woman scorned. Hiring a hit man was over the top, but would she have been justified in confronting Chanelle about what happened between Chanelle and Sean, even though it was months after the fact? Why?

6. Rick thought it was important for Chanelle to learn how to protect herself with a gun. What are your thoughts on using a gun for protection? Do you believe that women should know how to shoot a gun?

7. Chanelle may have been able to avoid a lot of pain that she caused herself if she was just honest with Rick about her past and the reasons why she was being stalked. If you were in Chanelle's shoes would you have told Rick or would you have tried to handle the problem yourself? Why?

8. Rick took Chanelle to Aruba, a romantic island that he used to visit with his wife. If you were Chanelle, how would you have felt about going to the same place that he took another woman that he once loved?

9. Rick and Chanelle's relationship moved very quickly. Do you think it's possible in real life to have an instant connection with someone and have your relationship move at warp speed? Discuss your answer.

CPSIA information can be obtained
at www.ICGtesting.com
Printed in the USA
LVOW04s1738021216

515533LV00009B/574/P